IT CAME FROM THE LOCH

MATTHEW MERCER

For My Father

"Something got to her. Something in the water. Something big."

Preface

When I started the "It Came From" series, I only planned for it to be a practice exercise while I figured out how this whole writing thing works. Through each of my books, I have tested many different processes, focused on learning specific aspects of writing, and figured out a whole lot more than I expected in this short amount of time. Still, I feel like I have no idea what I'm doing. I just sit at my computer, procrastinating for what feels like hours almost every day until some months go by and I have a script. Thankfully, I am noticing a significant improvement in quality from book to book, and I am so proud of the outcome of this one. This series has been incredibly fun to write, and I hope you guys have enjoyed the ride as much as I have. With that being said, I've gained enough confidence in my writing ability to move on from this series and work on a much bigger project; my first novel. I won't give anything away on that yet, but I promise you'll love that if you liked anything else I've written. As for this series, I have no plans to come back to it just yet; unless I find something experimental in my writing that I want to test. Until then, have fun with this story. It's a wild one, and my most experimental to date. Enjoy

Acknowledgement

I'll start by thanking my father, Walter, who I dedicated this book to. You were given the difficult task of raising not only me but my six siblings as well. To say we gave you a hard time would not even begin to cover the shit you've had to deal with over the years; but without the effort, time, care, and attention you've given all of us, we wouldn't have become who we are today. And, I quite like who I am, so thank you.

I have to thank my wife next, because without her, this whole thing wouldn't be possible. Working on these books for hours on end, day in and day out takes up *a lot* of my time—time that I could be focusing elsewhere. But, she recognizes what this means to me and not only puts up with it but helps make it work. Thank you for that.

I also have to give a special thank you to my editor, Danielle, who turned a script full of mistakes into something I can release with confidence.

To all the rest of my friends and family: thank you.

Lastly, I'm going to thank everyone that has ever either purchased or read one of my books. If you did both, you get an even bigger thank you. If you've bought and read all of them up to this point, wow. You're awesome. Keep it up. They only get better.

All of you make this worth doing, and turn what was just a simple hobby into something much more than that for me.

Thank you.

Content Warning

My books may contain graphic descriptions of death, gore, nudity, sexual situations, and many other potentially offensive situations. To keep from spoiling the contents of *this* book, I won't guarantee that everything listed above will be inside, but it might. If any of this offends you, or if you are uncomfortable with your child reading a story containing these contents, this might not be the book for you or them. Otherwise, enjoy the story.

Contents

Prologue

I t was a cold spring night out on the water. The breeze blew through young Elizabeth's scalp with grace. She stared outward, between the deck's guardrails, at the moon's reflection bouncing off the water. She closed her eyes and listened to the sounds of nature. She heard the waves crashing against the yacht, birds chirping overhead, the Scottish and American flags colliding as they flapped in the wind, and alcoholic laughter from the dining hall behind her.

She came out to the deck to escape the party and noise. Her family often overwhelmed her, and she liked isolating herself to calm her nerves. She understood they were on vacation, so she shouldn't be mad at them, but she had dealt with enough of their drinking problems at home and developed a hatred for it. However, being alone on a large body of water like this was much more exciting than her usual hiding place in her room.

At least, it *was* until her cousin Bradley stumbled his way onto the deck beside her.

Elizabeth could list her problems with alcohol for days: the sticky sweat that would paint itself on consumers' foreheads, the smell it left on their breath, the bottomless pit it left in her parents' wallets, but her biggest problem with it was how much it followed her. To her, no matter how much she avoided it, ran from it, hid from it, alcohol would always find her. For example, here she was, letting the adults have their fun, trying to get away from it all and enjoy nature, and out comes her least favorite co usin.

She had three cousins. First was Bradley, her oldest cousin, the son of her mother's brother, Roger. Then, Jamie and James were the twin siblings of her Aunt Christie on her father's side.

She wasn't close to any of them, but Bradley was her least favorite because he was the most inappropriate. She didn't think he meant any harm, but she was never comfortable around him.

Her parents would always excuse his poor behavior saying, "Don't mind him. He's just drunk." But that excuse didn't mean much to her because he was *always* drunk.

He took longer than he should have to reach the edge of the deck where she sat—the boat rocking didn't help his drunken knees. On top of that, he didn't seem to notice her presence. She was only eight years old and, therefore, small.

Elizabeth wasn't surprised, of course. She understood that Bradley's vision was impaired after too much drinking. Elizabeth was a precocious child. She worked hard in school, and living in a house with alcoholic parents, she spent plenty of her time learning to be independent. She often felt embarrassed by them and overcompensated with her education to *feel* like she was somehow better than them. However, all the knowledge in the world could not have prepared her for what Bradley would do next.

He stood next to her, his hip bone less than a foot away from her temple, unzipped his pants, placed his penis on the railing, and exhaled as he let out his hands-free piss stream.

To avoid having that image burned into her memory, Elizabeth forced herself to look away. She closed her eyes and pictured the moon's pretty reflection in the water.

"You're missing one *hell* of a party in there, girly," Bradley said as he shook off the last drops of urine.

So, he did know I was here. Elizabeth was preparing a response but lost it as a drop landed on her cheek. She had dealt with many disgusting things in her short life, but that moment shot to the top of her list. Her jaw would have hit the floor if she weren't afraid of catching another drop on her tongue. The voice of her parents saying, "he's just drunk," echoed around in her head, but it didn't help her. Nothing could. She waited for the sound of his pants zipper before she turned to face him.

He bent down, placing his hands on his knees to bring his head to her height. "How about I sneak you out some whiskey? It's pretty cold out here tonight. I'm sure that will warm you right up."

"Leave that little girl alone." Another man called from the dining room's entrance. It was her Uncle Roger, her favorite of her relatives.

"I'm just trying to cheer her up—"

"I don't care what you're doing," Bradley's father interrupted. "Get back in there and enjoy the party. Us sober folks need some time alone."

This was why he was her favorite. He hadn't always been, but for as long as she could remember, he was the sober one. Around the time she was born, Roger found himself hospitalized from alcohol poisoning. She heard from family members that he had a severe problem with drinking, in contrast to what they called their "social drinking." She would always roll her eyes at the thought. She didn't want to believe that the Uncle Roger she knew could be the worst of the family regarding alcohol, but he never denied the story and would even bring up how his liver almost gave out on him. But fortunately for him, he had a severe change in luck once he got out of the hospital; the difference being so intense that she imagined him getting whiplash from the events.

Once he could leave his house without assistance from another person, he found himself at the liquor store. He didn't have much left in his wallet, but he planned on using it to drink himself to sleep that night. Instead, he saw the sign for a lottery ticket in the window above the liquor store's entrance. He thought about it and made himself a promise. He would spend the last of his money on a chance for a better future, and if that opportunity presented itself, he would take it. And he did. The lottery ticket was a winner. Elizabeth wasn't sure of the exact amount, only that it was in the nine digits. Roger took it as a sign of *something* telling him to fix his life. He never drank another drop of alcohol. He struggled at first, especially at large family events and at home once Bradley grew old enough to drink. Being around so many others drinking made it hard for the recovering alcoholic not to. So, he took his money and moved to Scotland, leaving his adult son behind with his ex-wife. He left his entire family and the life he built in America and focused on his sobriety. Once he was stable enough, he bought out a luxury cruise line on Loch Ness and hired somebody to run it for him, providing a comfortable and steady income rather than a quickly depleting fund.

Elizabeth had gotten to know him after a few years had passed and he had enough confidence to fly to family functions and be in that environment without grabbing a bottle. Elizabeth always loved it when he came around because he would be the only family member that wouldn't stumble over drunken words. She could hold an actual conversation with him and would still remember it the next day. He made her feel safe.

That brings us to today. Roger wanted to celebrate five full years of sobriety by inviting his entire family to see his home, an expensive hillside mansion—a castle he liked to call it—overlooking Loch Ness. He paid for all their flights and promised to keep them all fed during their stay.

Now, as they all celebrated on the loch aboard one of her uncle's yachts, Elizabeth was with the most family members she had ever met.

Bradley looked back at her. His breath was visible as it traveled warmly through the cold air to her face.

She hated the smell of it.

"Don't have to tell me twice." Bradley stood upright and walked as straight as he could to the dining room.

"That son of mine." Roger shook his head and sat down beside her. "He didn't bother you too much, did he?"

Elizabeth shook her head, "No." She wanted to seem strong to her uncle but couldn't hold back her instinct to rub her face with her bicep, hoping she'd wiped her cousin's bladder fluids clean.

The boat rocked beneath them, this time more aggressive than it usually would against the waves, but they paid it no mind.

"Are you having fun out here? In Scotland, I mean." Roger asked.

Elizabeth nodded, "Yes."

"This is probably your first time out of the country, right? What do you think?"

"The people here talk funny!" Elizabeth giggled.

"They do, don't they?" Roger chuckled. "Don't go telling that to their faces." He shook his hand through her hair, making a mess of it. He looked toward the water. "It's beautiful, isn't it?"

She looked out the same way he did, really taking in the sight this time. "Mesmerizing," she said. It was a new word to her, and she was excited to use it.

"There she is!" Her mother's voice called from behind them.

"Are you enjoying the lake out here, Lizzy?" Her father, Jared, followed.

"It's called a loch!" Elizabeth said.

Her parents shared looks of amusement.

"She's right, you know?" Roger said. "Loch Ness."

"Well, *excuse* us!" Her mother said.

"Are you enjoying *Loch Ness*, Elizabeth?" Her father said.

"It's really pretty."

"It is, isn't it?" Her mother said.

Elizabeth was impressed with how composed the two of them were. She figured they would both be plastered by this time of night. Her father's tie would be undone, his upper buttons unbuttoned, and her mother would have taken her heels off by now. She assumed they would have found their way to their bedroom below deck and fallen asleep, forgetting about their daughter—their only responsibility. She wasn't wrong to have these assumptions because they all came from past experiences. But she was disappointed in herself for thinking so negatively of her parents.

"I think we are going to call it an early night tonight. Most of the others are finding their way to their rooms if they haven't already passed out at their tables, and we have to get up early enough to prepare for our flight home. Why don't you come inside and say good night to everyone before we go to bed?" Her mother reached out her hand to help Elizabeth up.

"Nonsense, Monica. Who knows how long it will take until she gets to come back here again? I won't always be able to pay for everybody's flights. Let her stay out with me for a little while longer. I'll make sure she gets to your room safely," Roger said.

Monica looked at her husband as though she were asking for his approval of her brother's idea.

"That should be fine. But not too late." He raised his finger, pretending to be stern with him; he then laughed it off, took his wife by the arm, and led her downstairs. The yacht shook aggressively again, causing the married couple to white-knuckle grip the handrail to stop themselves from falling.

"Are you guys okay?" Roger asked them.

Elizabeth's father responded with a simple thumbs-up and continued down the steps.

"Is the boat supposed to shake like that?" Elizabeth asked.

"Of course it is!" Roger sounded cheery, but his face didn't seem so sure. "It's just what happens when the waves push us around."

"But, that strongly?"

"Waves are like people," Roger said.

Elizabeth tilted her head in curiosity.

"They aren't all the same size. For example, you are tiny. I am rather normal, at least I'd like to think so. Then, there's your Aunt Christie. She would be one of the waves causing the boat to shake like that," Roger said with a smile.

Elizabeth burst into laughter. Her Aunt Christie was a lovely lady, but she was often the butt of many heavy-set jokes from her Uncle Roger. She overheard him tell a joke about her one Thanksgiving, and he's been making them ever since he saw the way it made her laugh.

The laughing stopped when another shaking of the yacht occurred, this time more violent than the rest.

Elizabeth and her uncle lost their balance; Elizabeth fell backward hard enough to slam her head onto the wooden deck floor. If the ringing in her ears wasn't already enough noise for her new headache, her drunken family's screams made it worse.

"That one wasn't Aunt Christie," Roger said, rubbing his eyes as he sat back up. "Shit, Lizzy, are you okay?"

Elizabeth prepared to nod, but the yacht shook again with a voluminous thud before a surge of water crashed against the right side of the boat.

"Get inside!" Roger yelled, struggling to stand.

Elizabeth got up from the deck and started to walk toward the dining hall, looking back to ensure her uncle was on his feet.

He was, only he wasn't following her inside. Instead, he looked over the boat's guardrail to see what was causing the ruckus.

"Do you see something?" Elizabeth's Aunt Tabitha asked from the upper deck above the dining room.

"Nothing at all!" Roger saw that Elizabeth was still waiting for him in the doorway near the dining room. "What are you doing? Get inside!" He pointed to the door behind her and ran across the deck to the other side to peer over the edge.

Whatever it was, the hit came from the back of the yacht this time; it knocked the boat upwards at a steep enough angle to knock Tabitha over the railing, where she fell almost twenty feet onto the deck below and landed on her neck in front of Elizabeth.

Elizabeth screamed while her uncle watched in terror. He ran to Tabitha's side and yelled at Elizabeth, "Don't look at her! Find your parents!"

Elizabeth didn't object. She ran into the dining room, past family members screaming and stampeding in different directions. Some to the left, others to the right, and the few who saw the fall ran past Elizabeth to check on Tabitha. They all had to maneuver around knocked-over tables, chairs, and broken shards from the dishes they had been served.

Elizabeth made it to the stairs on the left side, which she knew would take her to the room where her parents were supposed to be. But, half a dozen members of her family, most that she didn't recognize, blocked the stairs. At the bottom of the stairs was Jamie, the female of her twin cousins. Her Aunt Christie was attending to her daughter's swollen ankle. Next to them, Jamie's shoe lay on the floor with a broken heel.

She must have fallen.

Something slammed the side of the ship closest to them, splashing water over the railing and drenching everyone near the bottom of the stairs. The family screamed, echoing in the stairwell and filling Elizabeth's young ears with a ringing that she shouldn't have expected for another fifteen years, *at least.* Rather than waiting for Jamie and Christie to move out of the way, they stormed over them. Some could not proceed without trampling them. Elizabeth noticed more than one person stepping directly onto Jamie's injured ankle, but nobody cared. They couldn't.

Elizabeth was scared herself, but she was small enough to squeak past them without further injury once the rest of the family had cleared the walkway. As fast as her little legs would carry her, slipping once on the wet floor along the way, she ran to the back of the yacht where her room was. She swung the door open and found her parents inside. Her father was on the floor, his right leg pinned beneath an eight-drawer, vertical dresser that must have fallen over while the boat shook.

Her mother struggled to lift the dresser off him. She turned around once Elizabeth entered the room and looked relieved, given the circumstance. "Oh, honey, you're okay! Thank God. Please, help me lift this. I just need a little more room."

Without question, Elizabeth ran to the top end of the dresser while her mom lifted it from the side. Elizabeth put both hands on the back and used all the strength her body could muster, her feet sliding against the carpet as she pushed.

Her mother grunted and her father screamed in pain, but once his leg was free to move, he slipped out from underneath, and they dropped the dresser. It slammed loudly against the carpet and her mother rushed to his side, where he leaned against the bed's footboard.

"What the *fuck* is happening?" He asked.

"We need to go make sure everyone else is okay," Monica said.

Elizabeth wanted to object. She felt safer inside. But the boat was slammed again before they could get up from the floor. This time, it was met with mixed sounds of metal screeching and glass shattering.

Elizabeth's parents took her by the hand and escorted her out of the room. They went around the back corner where the rooms were aligned, toward the back of the boat, where there was another set of stairs. Only, this time, there wasn't.

They had to come to a screeching halt, her mother losing her footing on the wet wooden boards and slipping to her butt, only inches away from a giant hole in the floor that everyone saw for the first time, her high heels falling off her feet and into the water below. Everything was gone from the railing, across the walkway, and into the wall. They could see the floor below, filled with storage boxes of alcohol and fresh produce. They could also see into the empty bedroom, now soaked and missing the same dresser that every room had, identical in style to the one that had fallen on Elizabeth's father.

"Did we hit something?" he asked, lifting his wife to her feet.

"There's nothing here!" She yelled.

"Where's your brother?"

"He's probably still at the front deck," Elizabeth said.

"Shit!" Her father said, looking into the room below.

Elizabeth leaned her head as far as she felt comfortable. She could see the water begin to fill the room.

"The boat's going to sink," Monica said.

"Come on. We have to go tell everyone else." Her father took both of them by the hands, ran them back down the walkway Elizabeth had run through earlier, and screamed, "We're sinking!" along the way.

Elizabeth could hear her family gasping through their open bedroom doors and asking, "What?" as they ran past. Finally, they made it up the stairs; Jamie and Christie were no longer blocking the way.

Inside the dining room, Roger sat with James, the male twin. They both seemed devastated, and Elizabeth knew why once she saw Tabitha outside the dining room's entrance door, covered in a white tablecloth. She had died.

"What happened?" Monica asked. Her fear had turned to confusion.

"I'm sorry. I couldn't help her." James said.

"No, it's not your fault." Roger's voice cracked as he put his hand on his shoulder.

"What, who is it?" Monica asked.

"Aunt Tabitha," Elizabeth said.

Monica looked at her daughter, her eyebrows narrowed, then back to her brother. She realized that it was true by the look on Roger's face. "What? No...." She gasped and looked back at Elizabeth. "And you saw? Oh my...." Monica looked at her daughter as her eyes filled with tears. She started to run, but Roger yelled.

"Don't!"

Monica stopped.

"It isn't pretty. Just ... don't," he said.

Monica fell to her knees, but it didn't last long as the boat rose from its front end.

"I'm sorry, but we don't have time," Jared said.

Roger and James stood up, holding their hands at awkward angles like it was helping them balance.

"There is a big hole in the back of the ship. It is filling with water, and we are going to sink soon. We need to get off the ship," Jared said.

Elizabeth admired how calm her father was in this situation. She was glad he seemed sober enough to make this situation less scary for everyone involved.

Roger nodded and helped Jared lift Monica. They went outside to the bow, where most of the family ran from every different direction. Everyone was a mess. They were all confused and scared, some screaming, most asking what was happening, none having answers.

They all leaned over the front handrail and looked into the water for an answer. To their shock, they finally saw something—a shadow. It was hard to determine the shape, it was dark outside, and the water was dark enough. But undeniably, something was moving below them, and it was big.

If they didn't have enough problems, the boat was hit again, from below, directly in the ship's center. Horizontally across, from one end to the other—the boat split.

"Grab the ledge!" Roger yelled.

Elizabeth listened, but not everyone else did. Both the bow and stern were lifting, slowly morphing into a V-shape in the water. Elizabeth heard her family screaming as they slid down the deck toward the water. She was too scared to look behind her, telling herself:

Don't look down.

She listened to her advice until she saw James's fingers slipping off the railing to her right. She couldn't help but keep her eyes on him when he fell. Only he didn't fall into the water. Instead, he slammed into the glass window of the dining room, shattering it and disappearing deeper into the ship.

"Pull me up!" Monica yelled.

Elizabeth looked to her left side now, where her father was hanging from the railing, and her mother was hanging onto his ankle, dangling beneath him. The boat's bow was now pointing straight into the air, and her mother was parallel with what should have been the deck's floor.

"I'm trying!" Jared yelled, lifting his knee as high as he could, but he was clearly in pain as his wife's weight was pulling on the same leg he had just injured beneath the dresser.

"Mommy!" Elizabeth yelled before everything stopped. Or, at least, that's how it felt when her dad lost his grip on the railing, and both of her parents descended—in what felt like slow motion—into the water below. Elizabeth couldn't scream. She couldn't move a muscle. The whole world went dark, and she felt numb. She hung there for an eternity, waiting for her parents to emerge from the water.

She got her hopes up when she saw *something* rising, but it wasn't them. Instead, it was her Aunt Christie and her cousin,

Jamie. And they were dead. She felt like she was sinking, living an actual nightmare. It took her Uncle Roger, hanging from the same railing as her parents were hanging, to bring her back to e arth.

"Lizzy!" He yelled, snapping her out of the trance. "Your parents will be *fine*. But I need you to listen to me. Are you listening?"

Elizabeth nodded but kept averting her eyes to look down for her parents.

"I need you to hang on. Don't let go no matter what, you hear me? Quit looking down there. Look up and focus. You have to hold onto this railing until your feet touch the water. When they do, let go and swim to shore. Do you understand?" He asked.

Elizabeth swallowed her fear and nodded.

"Say it!"

"I understand," she said.

"Okay, close your eyes if you need to, but do *not* look down."

"Okay." She said and looked forward to the deck floor. "I'm scared."

"I know, sweetie. Me, too. But you will be okay. I promise," he said.

Elizabeth closed her eyes and started counting. It was how she would calm herself when she was stressed and how she fell asleep most nights when her parents were drunk and loud outside her bedroom door. But this time, she didn't wish for better parents. She didn't wish for a happy family like she often would. She didn't wish for a better life. She wished for her *parents'* safety. She wished for *her* life to be the same a week from now as it was before this trip. She focused on her wishes and tried to picture her life as a happy one, ignoring the screams of her family in the water from the opposite end of the boat. She heard water splashing to her left.

"Holy shit!" Roger yelled, followed by even more splashing, this time close to her, but Elizabeth kept her eyes closed.

With that splashing came an abundance of water, drenching her backside. She wanted to open her eyes and look, but she focused all her energy on maintaining her grip on the railing, that same grip now covered in freezing-cold water, the only plus side being that the numbness of her hands was better than pain.

Completely unaware of how much time had passed, she felt the water climbing up her foot to her ankle. Finally, it was time to let go.

She opened her eyes and looked to her left for her uncle. She wanted his approval to jump in the water, primarily because she remembered now that she didn't know how to swim. That wasn't her problem, though. No, her problem was that her uncle was gone. She looked all around, and none of her family could be seen.

The other half of the yacht was now entirely submerged. The water seemed empty behind her; she was a half-mile away from shore and alone.

She continued hanging onto the railing for as long as she could, only letting go once her head had fully submerged. She tried to recall every swimming instruction she had ever been given, but nothing worked. She waved her arms, kicked her legs, and, as much as she could, she tried to relax. Everything she tried made her sink faster.

She wasn't ready to give up, but she felt like this was it. She thought it was unfair. *I'm only eight years old*, she told herself. *I don't deserve this.* Her body was now as numb as her fingers were. She thought fear was an emotion she hadn't gotten to know too well by now, but this was something else entirely.

She eventually ran out of air, and as a reflex, she tried to inhale. Naturally, her throat flooded with water from the loch. Her family had teased her before they entered the yacht with stories about a monster that lurked beneath the depths. Some prehistoric dinosaur survived all of the meteors, and only a few lucky people have spotted it. She didn't buy any of it. She was too smart for that. At least, that was what she thought. But now, she wasn't so sure. What else could have attacked them like this?

She screamed a silent, breathless scream into the water when something wrapped around her waist, just below her navel. She looked down for the monster, but everything below her was black. She couldn't even see her own hands that punched her attacker. However, this didn't hurt like she thought being eaten alive would. It didn't hurt at all! The moonlight started reaching her head and filling out her body. Whatever *it* was, it was bringing her to the surface! She felt herself getting lightheaded from a lack of oxygen.

When she finally emerged from the depths, she spat out all the water that filled her mouth and coughed up more. Then, she took the deepest breath she ever had, and her savior emerged below her.

It was her cousin Bradley. For the first time, she was happy to see him.

He matched her deep inhale and wiped his hair out of his eyes. "Are you okay?"

Elizabeth kept silent. It was obvious that she wasn't okay. None of this was okay. But she couldn't find the proper vocabulary to express her emotions to him at that moment.

"Can you swim?"

She shook her head, "No."

"Okay, I will just have to carry you," he said.

She hugged him tightly and watched their backs as he swam toward shore. She watched as the last of the yacht sank below the water's surface.

"I got stuck in the dining room. I was behind the bar when the boat broke apart," he said.

Of course you were, she thought, but she couldn't stay mad at him. Not now. He was all she had left. She turned her head toward the beach they approached and saw the flashing red lights from the fire trucks speeding down the hill toward them. *You're too late*, she thought. *They're all gone.*

"Shit!" Bradley yelled, looking backward as he swam.

Elizabeth felt the water around her rising. She felt her cousin trying to pick up the pace as he swam. Looking back, she saw a wave coming for them, but it wasn't natural. The water was rising with *something* swimming toward them, and it was coming fast.

As if her heart wasn't beating fast enough, Elizabeth screamed when something surfaced beside her. It wasn't what was coming for them, however. Instead, it was much smaller, significantly less frightening, and equally as afraid of the wave of the unknown as she was. It was a turtle, larger than any she had seen at the local pet stores. It was almost the same size as Elizabeth, and it was swimming to shore alongside them.

Elizabeth looked back to the wave again; it was much closer, only feet away from them now. Then, the wave opened up, and Elizabeth stared into a gaping mouth.

Bradley screamed in her ear and let her go, pushing her forward.

With her quickest reflexes, she grabbed the turtle's shell and hoped it would support her weight while it continued to shore. When she felt comfortable upon its back, she looked back for the wave, and it was gone. There was no sign of her cousin. His screams were now silenced, and she was officially alone. She fell asleep on the turtle's back. The sound of the waves crashing onto the shore woke her up. She made it.

Chapter 1

The Flight

"**M**ommy!" Hailey tugged at her mother's shirt sleeve. "Mommy, I can't find Lana!"

Elizabeth stowed her carry-on bag beneath her uncomfortable airplane seat, then turned to face her daughter, who frantically rummaged through her bright-pink backpack. "Are you sure you packed her, baby?"

Lana was Hailey's favorite stuffed animal. She was a stuffed plesiosaur that her mom gifted to her for her first birthday. Hailey called her Lana because pronouncing "Loch Ness Monster" was too hard for a toddler. Elizabeth tried to help her with the pronunciation, and when that wouldn't work, tried to convince her that "Nessie" was a more fitting name, but Lana was the name that stuck.

"Yes, I'm sure! She was in my bag!" Hailey said.

Elizabeth spotted tears in Hailey's eyes. "I must have put her in your luggage before we boarded. I'm sorry. I will grab her as soon as we land. I promise."

"But I need her for the ride! And what if she's not there? Can you just grab her? The plane isn't moving yet."

Elizabeth loved how smart her daughter was, but she always admitted that it could be inconvenient in times like this. "I know the plane hasn't moved yet, but it's about to. Do you see that light up there?" Elizabeth pointed to the overhead "fasten your seat belt" light above them.

Hailey nodded yes.

"That means our seat belts must be on, so we won't fly away when the plane starts! I've got mine on." Elizabeth tugged at her belt. "Now, you don't want to fly away, do you?"

Hailey giggled and nodded yes again.

Elizabeth smiled back and shook her hand through Hailey's hair, making a mess of it. "No you don't, silly. Now, help me with your belt."

Hailey pulled the strap from beside her right hip across her belly. Elizabeth grabbed it from her, then clicked it in.

Hailey's smile had faded. "I still want Lana."

"I know, but there's nothing I can do, baby. She is safe in our luggage right above us, I promise."

"I didn't even want to go on this trip." Hailey crossed her arms and sunk into her seat.

"I know, but I couldn't just leave you at home! Everybody is coming on this trip with us, and I am *not* paying for a babysitter." Elizabeth brushed Hailey's hair back to normal using her fingers. Hailey's hair was Elizabeth's favorite feature because it was blonde and wavy like hers. It was her only feature that didn't remind Elizabeth of Hailey's father, who was never in the picture.

Elizabeth met him when she was a senior in college, and she had some time off for her winter break. Instead of relaxing and unwinding from her weeks of finals, she took the opportunity to party with friends. Which wasn't much different from her usual schedule during school, but the free time made her feel like she had more freedom to drink carelessly without consideration of repercussions.

The night itself was a blur. To this day, she can only remember brief glimpses of him buying her a drink, taking him back to her dorm, slipping off her top, and her friend, Alexa, walking in on them while she was bent over the back of their living room couch. She also remembered, rather vividly, waking up alone the next morning, sick to her stomach, running to the bathroom wearing nothing but her left sock. She barely made it to the toilet in time before vomiting the contents of her stomach. She showered and ate the eggs Alexa had made to help cure her ha ngover.

When Alexa asked who the guy was from the night before, Elizabeth realized she hadn't gotten his name. By the time they went out drinking that night, she had forgotten about him entirely. The partying and hangovers continued for the next couple of weeks. When she returned to school, she slowed down on drinking, but the sickness continued every morning. When she had her positive pregnancy test, she thought back to the one guy she had "gotten lucky" with and how *unlucky* she was not to have the slightest clue as to how she would contact him.

During her second trimester, she found his name. Christopher Atkins. It was just below a picture of his mug shot on the local news, stating that he was wanted for murder. Elizabeth spent the length of her pregnancy keeping up with the trial. He pled innocent, but the evidence was enough to convince Elizabeth that he would never meet his child, regardless of the verdict. When he was found guilty, she felt happy that she wouldn't need to keep him out of Hailey's life, but the sadness of raising a child without a father quickly set in. She weighed her options from abortion to adoption; it was too late for the former, and because she grew up in and out of foster homes as a child, the latter was not something Elizabeth would ever subject a child to. She decided that she was going to figure out the whole single mom thing, and she was going to kill it.

She finished college just before giving birth and became a self-employed marine biologist whose income was enough to keep her and Hailey fed with a roof over their head. At times, while they traveled around the United States, studying various aquatic anomalies, that roof was a hotel room.

Usually, her friends Brooke and Marcus, a young couple she had been friends with since college, would happily watch Hailey while Alexa and Elizabeth were out of town on a job. Since they were leaving the country for this next job, not only was Elizabeth uncomfortable being so far from Hailey, but Brooke and Marcus insisted on joining them on the trip.

"Is Alexa gonna be there too?" Hailey asked. She wasn't a fan of Alexa, and Elizabeth knew it. Hailey always considered her a bad influence on her mother because, more often than not, they were drinking when Hailey saw them together. Elizabeth knew from experience that it wasn't fun for a kid to be around a drinking parent, but Alexa was her college drinking partner and now her work partner. Old habits die hard.

"Of course she is. We've got work to do."

Hailey rolled her eyes.

"But you know who else is gonna be there?" Elizabeth said.

"Who?"

"Marcus. He's your favorite, right?"

"No!" Hailey turned to the window, but not before Elizabeth saw her blush. Marcus was often the one that Hailey would gravitate toward when Elizabeth's friends would come over. And when she would leave Hailey at Brooke and Marcus's apartment for a work trip, Marcus would make jokes about Hailey being his mistress and that she needed to keep it a secret from Brooke. The jokes were mostly harmless until they noticed Hailey started crushing on him.

Elizabeth asked him to tone down the jokes, so Hailey didn't start believing them. He obliged as best as he could, but he naturally emanated a certain confidence that attracted women. Even Elizabeth had a thing for him when they met in a class but backed off once she met Brooke.

"Whatever you say," Elizabeth said, turning her head to the flight attendant walking down the aisle, pushing a cart full of small plastic cups and various drink options.

"Can I get you guys something to drink?" She asked. She seemed young, either fresh out of college or still attending. She spoke with a calm, professional voice.

"What do you think, Hailey? Do you want some apple juice?" Elizabeth asked.

"Yes, please!" Hailey said.

"One apple juice, coming right up." As the flight attendant leaned into her cart to grab the juice, Elizabeth read "Sarah" on her name tag. "And how about you?"

"Can I get a vodka cranberry?" Elizabeth held her hand by her mouth and whispered to keep Hailey from hearing.

"Yes, of course. Can I see your ID?" She poured Hailey's drink and passed it to Elizabeth, who handed it to Hailey.

"My seven-year-old daughter isn't enough proof?" She joked, reaching into her purse before handing over her driver's license.

"Well," Sarah scanned the license, "Elizabeth. I have one of my own, and I know how exciting it is when people still think *I* look twenty years old." She handed the license back to her and pulled out the vodka.

"Ah, so it was a compliment, then?"

Sarah nodded, handed her the drink, and held out a tablet with an attached credit card reader.

"Can you keep a tab? If so, keep coming around throughout the flight, and we will get to know each other well."

"Yeah, I can do that." Sarah smiled, nodded, and continued down the aisle.

Above them, the speakers made a *ding*, and a voice rang through after. "Good evening, this is your pilot speaking. You are on board flight 410, departing from San Francisco en route to Lincoln, Nebraska."

Elizabeth sat confused and silent with the rest of the passengers until he spoke again,

"I'm only kidding. Trust me; nobody wants to go to Nebraska. We will arrive at your destination in Scotland in approximately twelve hours. It's a long flight, so feel free to get up now and then to stretch your legs, but keep an eye on that seat belt light, because we don't want anybody to get hurt. Turbulence is no fun, and we will face plenty of it. Otherwise, take a nap, and don't cause any trouble for my lovely flight attendants." He drew a blush and smile from the elder of the crew as she walked by. "Have a safe flight."

Scotland. More importantly, Loch Ness. It had been over twenty-two years since Elizabeth's family tragedy, and she had mixed feelings about returning. She spent her life studying marine biology, hoping to find an answer to what happened that night, but there had been no luck. Whenever she would have a theory that failed, she would joke with herself: *Maybe it was just the Loch Ness monster.* But everything she ever learned about marine life would constantly disprove the possibility of a creature of that size living in that small body of water.

However, she recently stumbled upon an article that drew her attention. The title was "An Influx of Non-Native Sea Turtles Found in Loch Ness." This article brought her back to the night of the tragedy, where, as she remembers it, a giant turtle had saved her life. Jumping at the opportunity for a potential breakthrough in her research, she called Alexa and told her they were going to Scotland.

Researching foreign turtles wasn't the most exciting job offer, but Alexa wouldn't be working without Elizabeth. She booked the first flight she could, and Alexa booked hers with Brooke and Marcus. She studied up on those turtles in her free time before the flight and developed a theory regarding why they were there now and why they were also there the night of her accident. To save herself from the embarrassment of her friends thinking she was insane, she opted not to share her theory.

"Peanuts?" Sarah asked, startling Elizabeth, who had started to doze off.

"What?" Elizabeth asked.

"Would you like some peanuts?"

"Sure, why not?"

Sarah handed her two small packs, and Elizabeth put them on the small, retractable table in front of Hailey, who was already asleep.

"Would you like to order some food?" Sarah asked.

"Oh, can I see a menu?"

"Yes, of course." She pulled out a menu from the side of her cart and handed it to her.

"So, how long will you guys be in Scotland? I'm always curious about flight attendants who work international flights," Elizabeth asked while reading the menu.

"Just a night or two before we work the next flight back to the States."

"That sounds like a long time."

"It is, but we treat it like a vacation."

"Oh, that sounds fun. What do you usually do while you wait to get back on the plane?"

"I get along pretty well with my coworkers, so we usually find a nice bar or restaurant and hang out there. What about you? What's the occasion?"

"I'm studying turtles." Sarah pointed at the menu, "Can I have the steak and potatoes?"

"Sure. What about your daughter?"

"She will probably ask for mac and cheese when she wakes up in a few hours."

"Alright, I'll be back with that once we are at a comfortable altitude. And I'll have some questions about those turtles."

"Thank you, Sarah."

"Flight attendants, prepare for takeoff." The pilot's voice rang through the speakers.

Sarah smiled, walked her cart to the front of the plane, put it away, and fastened her seat belt.

Elizabeth held on to her and Hailey's cups during the takeoff process. Her heart would skip a beat, once when they started accelerating and once again when they left the ground.

Once they were in the air, she checked to ensure Hailey was okay, downed her drink in two gulps, and dozed off.

Chapter 2
Arrival

The final few hours of the flight were the worst. Elizabeth got most of her sleeping done early, so she was awake for all the bad parts: turbulence, crying babies, occupied bathrooms. Their food was decent, but Hailey wasn't a fan of hers. However, Elizabeth believed she wouldn't have been a fan of anything she was given because she didn't have Lana.

Once they landed, Elizabeth pulled their luggage from the overhead bin, opened up Hailey's, and sure enough, Lana was waiting for her.

Hailey ripped her from her mother's hands, squeezed her, and smiled so big that Elizabeth forgot about her daughter's twelve-hour fit during the flight.

"Have fun out there," the flight attendant, Sarah, said while Elizabeth exited the plane.

"You too. Maybe we will run into each other," Elizabeth said. They exchanged goodbye nods, and Elizabeth continued through the airport toward the exit. She pulled her phone out of her purse and checked the time. It read 10:15 a.m., but the sun setting through the windows reminded her that jet lag would be a problem here. She scanned the walls for the first clock she could find, and the hands pointed at 6:15 p.m.

She found Alexa's name in her contacts and pressed the call button, only to be reminded she would not have service here. *Everyone I know will be with me. Why would I pay for roaming service?*

It seemed like a good idea at the time, but she hadn't thought about how she would find them once she got to the airport.

"Where are we going?" Hailey rubbed her eyes. Her hair was a mess.

"We have to find everyone else, sweetie," Elizabeth said.

"Are they here already?"

"They should be. They should've landed a couple of hours before we did."

They exited the airport and looked around the pick-up section of the sidewalk, hoping to see one of her friends, but she didn't. A car horn echoing beneath the overhead cement parking structure startled them. It came from an all-black Range Rover that pulled up beside them. The front window on the right side of the vehicle rolled down, and Elizabeth recognized Marcus behind the steering wheel as he peeked his head out the window. This car was different from those she was used to; the steering wheel was on the opposite side of the vehicle.

"Need a ride?" He asked and waved his fingers at Hailey.

"Yes, please," Elizabeth said. The car trunk popped open; Elizabeth walked to the back and placed her bag in the trunk before helping Hailey do the same. Over the seats, she could see Alexa sitting in the back right seat, and Brooke was sitting in the passenger seat to the left of Marcus.

Elizabeth led Hailey around the left side of the car and opened the door for her; she climbed into the middle seat, holding Lana in her right arm. Elizabeth got in behind her.

"Took you guys long enough," Alexa said, smacking her chewing gum dramatically. She had pitch-black hair that she wore straightened and long down her back. Her caramel-colored skin exemplified her Hispanic ethnicity. She pulled her sunglasses up carefully with her recently manicured nails and rested them behind her hairline. She made it obvious through her appearance that she would treat this trip as more of a vacation than a job.

"She's joking. We only *just* got out of the car rental place," Marcus said. He seemed tired and dressed the part with his sweatpants and hoodie combo. He wore a beanie over his buzzed hair. "They took forever trying to figure out if my license was legit."

"Yeah, and that wasn't even the worst part. The guy's accent there was just *awful*. If they all talk like that, I might as well pack up and go home early," Alexa said.

"You think so? I thought it was kind of hot," Brooke said.

Marcus looked at her, disappointed.

"Well, you had perfect timing. I was going to freak out if I couldn't find you guys. I forgot that I couldn't use my phone here." Elizabeth said.

"Seriously, none of you guys listen to me," Brooke turned around in her seat to look at them, "I said it was a terrible idea to be in a foreign country and not have a way to communicate, but you guys just ignored me." She wore her hair in a ponytail and a sweatpants and hoodie outfit that matched Marcus's.

"Wait, nobody else paid for their phones either? I thought for sure Alexa would," Elizabeth said.

"What's that supposed to mean? I'm hoping to escape my at-home life while we're here," Alexa said.

"Bitch, we are your life," Brooke said and turned around to face the front. "You guys are gonna regret not having your phones, I promise."

"Okay, well, can you use yours to get us out of here?" Marcus said.

"Yeah, Elizabeth, give me the address," Brooke said.

"Check our group chat. It's the last thing I sent."

Brooke scrolled through her messages briefly and then opened her GPS app.

"Oh, it's only like thirty minutes from here. That's not too bad," Marcus said while Brooke positioned her phone on the holder she clipped onto the air-conditioning vent.

"Everyone has everything, right?" Marcus asked, and they all nodded. "Okay, let's get out of here." He put the car in gear and sped off.

Once Marcus was comfortable on the road and away from the airport parking lots, Alexa turned to face Hailey. "I see you brought Lana with you."

"Yep! She comes with me everywhere I go." She squeezed Lana against her chest.

"Well, did your mommy tell you where we are going on this trip?"

"Duh, we're in Scotland," Hailey said.

Brooke giggled from the front seat, and Alexa smiled at Elizabeth as if Hailey's innocence were too much for her to handle.

"Well, yes, but not only that! We are going to Loch Ness! Do you know where that is?"

Hailey shook her head no.

"Loch Ness is this huge lake out here in Scotland," Alexa made her voice deep and mysterious, "And in that lake is a big, scary monster."

Goosebumps shot up Elizabeth's arm, but Hailey seemed amused.

"What kind of monster?" Hailey asked.

"They call it the Loch Ness Monster. Some people call it Nessie for short. But we call it," Alexa tapped Hailey's stuffed animal on the nose, "Lana."

Hailey looked back to her mother, confused. "But ... I thought Lana was a dinosaur. And dinosaurs are extinct! There can't be one out here!"

"You are *so* smart, baby," Elizabeth said. "Dinosaurs *are* extinct, and there is no such thing as a Loch Ness monster. It's just something that people made up."

Hailey squeezed Lana even tighter, "How do we know there aren't dinosaurs in the water?"

"Because I study the water and its living creatures, sweetie."

"But we can never be too sure, can we? We are studying Loch Ness on this trip, so maybe we will find it," Alexa said.

Hailey's eyes widened.

"Of course, there's no dinosaur! The water is perfectly safe. People swim in it all the time! It's a huge tourist spot because of the legend. Everyone wants to see if they can find the monster, but nobody ever does. And after all these years, if some giant dinosaur lived in there, it would have been found by now," Brooke said.

"Even if there were some monster in there that has lived thousands of years out of its natural habitat, you wouldn't have to worry. I'll make sure nothing happens to you while I'm here, okay?" Marcus reached back and shuffled Hailey's hair. He lost his grip on the steering wheel for a brief second and jerked the car to the right, but Brooke was quick enough to catch the steering wheel and keep them in the lane.

"Hey, hands on the wheel!" Brooke said.

"You could've killed us!" Elizabeth said.

"I'll make sure nothing happens to you while I'm here, okay?" Alexa said, imitating Marcus.

"Geez, I'm just trying to comfort the girl. All this talk of monsters had her all worked up," Marcus said.

"Crashing the car isn't the best way to calm someone down," Alexa said.

"No, but it would shut you up."

"Just know that when I die, I will come back and haunt you." Alexa stuck her tongue out at him.

"Wouldn't that be a nightmare?"

"Both of you shut up. I think we're almost there."

2

The rest of the drive was slow and quiet, as everyone was tired from the flight. The GPS brought them up a long and windy road on a hillside. Once they reached the top of the hill, Brooke pointed out their first view of the loch beneath the rising moonlight.

"It's so pretty!" Hailey yelled, waking up a napping Alexa.

"Just like I remember it," Elizabeth whispered. The view of the moonlight on the water filled her with a nostalgic calmness, reminding her of the time before her tragedy.

"Wait, you've been here before?" Brooke asked.

"Yeah, a long time ago."

"I think this is it," Marcus said.

As they reached the top of the hill, they came across an old-timey mansion seated behind a stone wall and a black gate.

"No way, that's the house?" Brooke asked.

"More like a mansion," Alexa said.

"Actually, I think they called it a castle," Elizabeth said.

"I didn't know your family was filthy rich!" Brooke said.

"Not all of us. Just my cousin."

"What does he do? This is insane." Marcus pulled the rental car up to the gate and parked it.

"I can't imagine he does much these days. Around twenty years ago, there was an accident. His father died, and his yacht sunk. An insurance claim and an inheritance later, my cousin lives in a Scottish castle and is the proud owner of a popular yacht cruise line."

"Lucky him," Marcus said.

"Doesn't that sound like a dream? Not only a fat inheritance but a dead dad, too." Brooke said, her face chipper at the thought.

"Not everyone has daddy issues like you, Brooke," Alexa said.

"Will we be able to go on one of those cruises while we're here?" Brooke asked.

"I was planning on asking him, but I'm not so sure," Elizabeth said.

"So, do we just wait here, or—" Marcus was interrupted by the castle gate swinging open, inviting them inside. "I guess not."

Roughly one hundred yards of paved gravel road led them from the gate to the front of the castle, where a woman stood waiting by the open front door. She wore a green and white striped sundress with a thin, green, long-sleeved sweater and white flats.

"I'm gonna assume they were expecting us," Marcus said as he pulled the car up to meet her.

"Yes, they knew we were coming tonight," Elizabeth said.

Marcus rolled down the window as the woman approached the car. "Where should I park the car?"

"Right here is fine while you unload your bags," she spoke in a soft, calming voice with a familiar accent from the American west coast, "but our garage is around the side of the castle."

"Thank you." Marcus rolled up the window.

"She really called it a castle." Brooke unbuckled her seat belt.

"Told you," Elizabeth said as she unbuckled her seat belt before taking off Hailey's. She hopped out of the car and then helped Hailey out. Elizabeth walked around the back of the car and introduced herself to the woman. "Hi, I'm Elizabeth, Bradley's cousin."

"Oh, it's so nice to finally meet you!" She offered her hand, and Elizabeth shook it. "My name is Monica."

"Really? That was my mother's name." Elizabeth said while her friends exited the car and headed to the trunk to unload.

"Oh, she was your mom? Bradley told me that he had an aunt that shared my name." Monica reached out and caressed Elizabeth's arm, "I am sorry about what happened to your family. It was truly awful. I can't imagine it."

"Oh, thank you—"

"So why does *she* know what happened to your parents, and your best friends don't?" Brooke interrupted while struggling to pull her over-packed luggage from the trunk.

"They didn't know? Oh, I'm sorry." Monica said.

Elizabeth shook her head, "Because my cousin is apparently more open to talking about it."

"Then you *have* to tell us," Brooke said.

"Babe, stop." Marcus appeared from behind her and pulled her luggage out.

"If she doesn't say, we'll just ask her cousin."

"Okay, fine." Elizabeth walked to the trunk and pulled out Hailey's luggage before her own. "The accident on my uncle's yacht that I told you about. We were all on it."

Her friends stopped what they were doing and looked at her.

"All of you? You mean you were there too?" Alexa said.

"My whole family was," Elizabeth covered Hailey's ears, "and everybody died. Everybody except me and my cousin." She removed her hands from her daughter. "My cousin saved my life."

Her friends remained silent.

"Well, how about I show you all inside?" Monica asked. "I can grab your bag if you'd like." She reached her arm out to Hailey, who handed her the luggage she was dragging.

Marcus closed the trunk once they had removed everything, and with a *beep*, the car locked.

Monica started walking toward the open front door, and they all followed.

"Hey, Elizabeth," Alexa walked beside her and whispered, "I'm sorry to hear about what happened. I had no idea."

"Don't worry about it. It was a long time ago," Elizabeth said.

"Since you went through something so horrific here," Brooke spoke loudly from the back of the group, "why would you ever want to come back?"

They all stopped at the front door.

"I wanted to study the turtles," Elizabeth said.

Chapter 3

Pregame

"Oh!" Monica said, "I never got the rest of your names." She stepped into the doorway, lifting Hailey's luggage carefully over the half-step.

"I'm Marcus."

"Brooke."

"And I'm Alexa. I work with Elizabeth."

"And let me guess," Monica leaned down and handed Hailey her bag, "you're Hailey."

Hailey smiled and laughed, "How'd you know?"

"I have my ways," Monica stood up straight. "Okay, everyone, the rooms are this way." She led them through the foyer that looked bigger than Elizabeth's entire apartment. Paintings and candles decorated the walls with classy, beige and white wallpaper. Across from the entrance was a double staircase surrounding a hallway, with matching hallway entrances on both walls, to the left and right. Atop each side of the stairs stood prop suits of knights' armor, visible through the thick, white banister. Monica headed for the hallway straight ahead, but they all took their time to admire the room before following.

"This place is fucking huge," Brooke said.

"Hey," Marcus nudged her with his elbow, "show some respect."

"Sorry, it's fucking huge *and* spotless."

Marcus rolled his eyes, but she wasn't wrong. Elizabeth ran her fingers along the wooden frame of the sofa she stood beside. Somebody had polished it so she could see her reflection staring back at her.

"Thank you. I just cleaned it this morning, actually," Monica said, waiting by the entrance to the hallway.

"Wait, you cleaned this whole house by yourself?" Alexa asked from the grandfather clock in the corner between the right hallway entrance and the front door.

"I try my best to keep it up throughout the week, but when I heard that we were having guests for the first time in a long while, I may have tried a little harder."

"But you don't have any help?" Elizabeth asked.

"I don't need it. Bradley requested full-time services from me, so I live here Monday through Thursday. I have a room downstairs. And we don't get much company, *any* company really, so it's mostly just dusting and replenishing the bar."

"There's a bar?" Alexa asked, but Elizabeth didn't wait for an answer before her next question.

"So you've been working with Bradley for a while?"

"It's been a few years now. He's had other caregivers, but they could never handle him. He has a strong personality," Monica said.

Elizabeth nodded, thinking back on her many horrifying experiences with him.

"The hours were perfect for me, and living here most of the week was even better since my home is quite a distance away. And lucky for me, Bradley has done *a lot* of growing up since I started working for him."

"Thank God," Elizabeth said.

The group followed Monica down the hallway, stopping at the first door on the right. "This is my room. Bradley allowed me to work more hours this week, so I'll be here all weekend if you need anything. If you can't find me in the house, knock, and I'll likely be here."

"Sweet," Alexa said before they continued on. They stopped about twenty feet down the hall, where two doors stood across from each other.

"This door here would be the guest bathroom for the first floor," Monica opened the door on the right side and flicked the light switch on the inside, revealing a bathroom bigger than Elizabeth's bedroom at home. In the left corner sat a two-person, Jacuzzi-style bathtub with a separate shower beside it, surrounded by three glass walls and dark, marble-finished wall and flooring with a matching bench inside. To the right of the doorway was a long sink and countertop that was as polished and reflective as the rest of the house.

"If this door across from it is a bedroom, I'm taking it," Alexa said, pushing open the door on the left side of the hallway.

"Yes, that would be the first guest room," Monica said.

"I'm taking it." Alexa invited herself inside, flicked on the light switch, and tossed her luggage onto the king-sized mattress. The room was large, with a framed painting of the famous

Urquhart Castle covering most of the wall across from the door. On the right was a horizontal dresser with a TV on top of it.

"This room is nice," Marcus said.

"Does the TV work? Does he pay for cable here?" Brooke asked.

"No cable, but it is a smart TV, so you can probably find something on the streaming apps. Try them out, and I'm sure you'll find something that works." Monica said.

"I hate to do this," Alexa unzipped her luggage, "but I was on that plane for *way* too long, so these clothes need to come off. Unless you wanna see that, I suggest you get out of here."

"Oh, alright then." Monica turned around and left the room.

Elizabeth walked Hailey out behind her, and Brooke pushed Marcus through the doorway and shut the door.

"This door on the left is the second bedroom." Monica stepped to the next door and opened it, flicking on the light switch upon entering. "Brooke and Marcus, if I'm not mistaken, the two of you are together, right?"

"That's right," Marcus said.

"Unless I find a cute enough Scottish guy while I'm here," Brooke said.

"I find that ... unlikely. In any case, this will be your room. It has a large enough bed for the two of you, and I have already prepared the other room down the hall with an extra bed for Hailey, so they wouldn't have to share. But if you'd rather, I can fix up another room for the two of you to sleep separately," Monica said.

"The one room will be fine," Marcus said.

"We'll see how the trip goes," Brooke quipped.

Monica stepped out of the room and allowed Brooke and Marcus inside.

"This room is insane," Marcus said. "I can't believe people live in places as big as this."

"The perks of your family dying, I guess," Brooke said.

"Funny," Elizabeth remarked, "Bradley got a castle, and I got a foster home."

"Your room will be just down the hall," Monica gestured to the door at the very end of the hallway.

"Okay, well, I'm gonna put Hailey to bed, and I'll come find you guys after," Elizabeth said.

Brooke collapsed beside Marcus on the bed and gave her a thumbs-up.

"Follow me, then," Monica said, leading the way down the hall to the final door.

She held the door open for them, the light inside already emanating from a pull-string lamp beside the larger bed on the left side of the room. To the right was the smaller twin bed Monica had set up for Hailey. Directly across from the door was a bay window with a clear view of the loch over the edge of the hill. To the left side of the smaller bed stood an open doorway with a bathroom inside, smaller than the one in the hallway.

"Oh, I must've left the light on! I was cleaning this room when you all pulled up to the gate."

"Oh yeah, how did you know when we arrived?" Elizabeth wheeled her luggage into the room and left it beside her new bed.

"Cameras. My phone alerts me whenever someone arrives." Monica said, watching Hailey enter the room and jump onto the bed, leaving her luggage to fall on the floor. "Well, I'll let you guys get settled in. If you need anything, just let me know."

"Of course, thank you. Oh, actually," Elizabeth caught her as she was exiting, "is Bradley here? I want to thank him for letting us stay here."

"He is here, but he is asleep in his room upstairs. I wouldn't wake him tonight. When he takes his nighttime pain medication, he crashes like he's been hit by a truck. It would only upset him if he were disturbed," Monica said.

"Okay, I'll catch up with him tomorrow, then. Thanks again."

"Of course." Monica patted the door and pulled it shut on her way out.

"So, what do you think, Hailey? Is this place awesome, or what?" Elizabeth asked.

"It's the best house ever!" Hailey threw her arms into the air and held them widely apart. "It's *so* big!"

"It is. My cousin is a lucky guy. I'll introduce you to him tomorrow, and you can tell him how much you like this place. He would love that."

"I get to meet another member of the family?" Hailey crawled to the edge of her bed and kicked her shoes off.

Elizabeth hadn't thought about it before, but this was the first time Hailey would ever meet another family member. It was upsetting, and she felt terrible that Bradley was the only one she would ever meet, given her negative experiences with him. But at least she got to meet *someone*. And, if what Monica said was true, maybe he had changed. Still, she knew to be wary of his behavior. She would always be protective of Hailey, but she had high hopes for now.

"Yeah, you do. Would you like that?" Elizabeth asked.

Hailey nodded.

"Okay, let's get you in your pajamas and get you to bed," Elizabeth said.

"But I'm not tired!"

"That's called jet lag. Back in California, it's daytime like we're used to, but it's night over here. You need to sleep to get used to the new time." Elizabeth picked up Hailey's luggage, placed it on the bed beside Hailey, and unzipped it.

"But I slept on the plane!"

"I know, baby, but you'll be fine. I promise."

Hailey rolled her eyes, grabbed her backpack and ran into the bathroom, closing the door behind her. Elizabeth dug through Hailey's luggage, pulled out a few options for her to sleep in, and laid them out on the bed. She heard the bathroom faucet turn on and the buzzing vibration of Hailey's toothbrush.

A gust of wind blew in from behind the rightmost curtain, drawing Elizabeth's attention to the window. The wind felt cold as it brushed against her ankle. She approached the window and pulled it shut, turning her attention to the view of Loch Ness.

She watched the waves crashing against the shore and studied the water, looking for any sign of something to answer her questions about what happened that night, knowing she wouldn't find any. Unsure of how long she stood there gazing out the window, Hailey broke her from the trance when she jumped onto the bed, already dressed in her onesie pajamas.

"Are you all ready to get tucked in?"

"If I have to," Hailey said.

"I know, sweetie. But you'll wake up early, and we will have fun tomorrow, I promise!" Elizabeth pulled the other pajamas off Hailey's bed and placed them on her luggage.

Hailey crawled beneath her covers and Elizabeth pulled them up to her neck.

"Get some sleep, okay? I'll be in here to sleep soon too." Elizabeth kissed her on the forehead.

"Good night," Hailey said.

"Good night, baby. I love you."

After tucking Hailey into bed, Elizabeth wandered out of her room and down the hallway to the front of the castle, where she heard a scream from the direction of the hall to her right. It led her to an open set of double doors; inside, she found Alexa, Brooke, and Monica sitting along a half-moon-shaped bar, with Marcus behind it pouring shots.

"I found the bar!" Alexa yelled, on the verge of falling out of her stool.

"It looks like you've already had enough," Elizabeth teased.

"I haven't even had my first." Alexa grabbed her glass from the group while Marcus pulled out a fifth glass and poured Elizabeth a shot of something dark.

"Then this is gonna be a long night." Marcus passed out the rest of the glasses and raised his own for a toast. "To our friends, old and new," he gestured his head to Monica, "to successful turtle studies and a lively, fun vacation."

"Cheers!" The group cheered and threw their shots back.

The warm liquid swam smoothly down Elizabeth's throat, leaving a deep burning in her chest that made her regret not asking for a chaser.

"Whoo!" Alexa cheered.

"Fuck," Marcus cringed and slammed his glass onto the counter, "that's what expensive bourbon tastes like?

"You're such a baby. Pour me another, Mr. Barkeep." Brooke said as she leaned backward from her seat, arching her back across the bar top and opening her mouth with a tongue-out smile.

Without hesitation, Marcus picked up the bottle and poured it into her mouth until she couldn't handle any more. She swung her body upright, choking and squirting the drink from her nose and swallowing what remained with two disgusted gulps.

"My turn!" Alexa replicated Brooke's pose, arching over the bar, sticking her tongue out to her chin, and closing her eyes.

"That fucking burns," Brooke said, tears forming in her eyes. "Close your mouth." She pinched Alexa's tongue with her index finger and thumb.

Alexa fell back into her seat and pouted. "You guys are no fun."

"This is more fun than I've had in a *long* time," Monica said.

"Really? Why?" Elizabeth asked. The burning had finally escaped from her chest.

"I'm a bit of a hermit. I don't have many friends, well, *any* friends. And I don't have any family, either. Just Bradley."

Sounds familiar, Elizabeth thought to herself.

"That sucks," Brooke said.

"I'm sorry to hear that. Your family must be in America, right?" Marcus asked. "I noticed you don't have an accent."

"And I'm *so* glad you don't," Alexa said.

"I think that's part of why Bradley likes having me around so much. I'm sure my lack of an accent reminds him of America. He misses it there."

"Are you sure it's not because you're easy on the eyes?" Brooke asked with finger quotes.

"Maybe, but I seriously doubt that. He has never made any advances that made me uncomfortable."

"Are you sure you're talking about *my* cousin Bradley?" Elizabeth asked. "As far as I can recall, he was always a creep."

"Oh, goodness, no. Bradley has always shown me nothing but kindness and respect."

Wow, maybe he really has changed, Elizabeth thought, swirling her empty shot glass around her finger on the bar top.

"As for my family, truth be told, I don't know where they are. I left America behind many years ago and haven't spoken to anyone since," Monica said.

"Why'd you leave?" Elizabeth asked.

"If it's okay, I'd rather not get into that. Bad memories. You know?"

"Of course," Elizabeth said, "don't worry about it."

"So, ladies, tell me. What is the plan for the evening?" Marcus asked, walking around the bar and sliding onto the stool beside Brooke.

"Is there an actual public bar around this place? It would be nice to dress up and have a night on the town," Alexa said.

"There's a nice bar close to the loch. I can give you the address if you have GPS," Monica offered.

"What, you won't come with us?" Elizabeth asked.

"It's getting a little late for me. Trust me, I would love to, but I've spent all day cleaning and have some things I need to finish before I go to sleep. But I'll go out with you guys another night," Monica promised.

"If that's the case, would you mind making sure Hailey is okay while we're gone?" Elizabeth asked. "She's asleep now, but I would feel safer knowing you'll keep an eye on her."

"Of course! You guys go have fun."

"Alright, let's get dressed." Brooke hopped off her bar stool and dragged Marcus out of the room. Elizabeth and Alexa followed them.

Chapter 4
Cheers to New Friends

"Alexa, I can see your nipples." Brooke laughed as Alexa entered the front room of the castle where they all had been waiting.

Alexa wore a plain white tank top beneath a lightweight, mid-length cardigan. As Brooke had pointed out, it was obvious she was not wearing a bra.

"Shut up. It's cold," Alexa said.

"You could wear something warmer," Elizabeth suggested.

"Or a bra, *at least*," Brooke snarked.

"Hey, my eyes are up here." Alexa pointed her index and middle fingers at her eyes and gestured back and forth between herself and Brooke.

"It's not *my* eyes I'm worried about." Brooke turned to Marcus, who held up his hands to maintain his innocence.

"Maybe if you let your tits hang out more, he wouldn't have to stare at mine."

"That's not the problem here," Elizabeth said.

"Look, you've already got a man to screw, Brooke. Some of us still have to put in work to make it happen."

"Yeah, but that doesn't mean every person in Scotland should see your tits for free. Wouldn't you want them to earn it?

Besides, look at Elizabeth. She's single *and* dressing like a re-spectable woman."

"My goal isn't to be *respected* at the bar. Now, are we going or not?" Alexa opened the door and stepped out.

"I'm not driving you to some dude's house later." Marcus stepped outside.

"We're not picking you up, either." Brooke followed.

"Don't even ask about bringing them here." Elizabeth turned to Monica, still inside, "Promise me you'll keep Hailey safe?"

"You have nothing to worry about. We'll all be sleeping safe and sound when you return," Monica assured.

"How will we get in?"

"I will leave the gate open, and I've already given Marcus the key to the front door. Oh, and that reminds me! When you pull in, drive around the castle's right side and you will find the driveway. If you need anything else, just call."

"Thank you," Elizabeth and Marcus said in unison.

Monica closed the door, and Elizabeth heard it lock. Marcus clicked the button on the key fob, and the car lit up when it unlocked its doors. He headed to the left side of the vehicle to get in but remembered that the steering wheel was on the opposite side; the girls watched him jog back to the other side and get in. Brooke got into the passenger seat. Elizabeth and Alexa hopped into the back. Marcus started the car.

"Here, I have the directions." Brooke brought out her phone and entered the bar's address that Monica provided into the GPS.

Marcus put the car into gear, and off they went.

"She wasn't joking when she said this was close to the loch," Marcus said, putting the car into park.

They were in the parking lot of a small pub with a bright sign that read, "The Loch-it Inn," with a heart-shaped locket design hanging from the hyphen. To their right, just past the road, was a five-foot, grassy decline to Loch Ness; where it met the water were tall shrubs visible from their car.

"Good thing. I'm going to need somewhere to go throughout the trip," Alexa said, hopping out of the car. The others followed. She rubbed her hands against her arms while they walked through the parking lot, shaking with the freezing temperature.

"I hope you're regretting your outfit," Brooke said.

"Why? Is Marcus still eye-fucking me?" Alexa asked, making Brooke's face go red.

Elizabeth and Marcus looked shocked, but both stayed out of it. Alexa approached the door to the pub, and upon opening it, all of the noise from inside poured out and filled the otherwise silent night.

The small and welcoming pub reminded Elizabeth of her favorite dive bars back home. They had a few scattered pool tables, numerous high-top tables with just enough distance from the pool tables for the players to walk around them, an oval-shaped bar in the center of the room, a dart board beside a jukebox playing 90s rock, and the TVs were playing some sport none of them recognized. They all followed Marcus to the bar.

"Four shots of tequila, please," Marcus told the bartender.

"Make it five, and they're on me," a female voice called behind them. It took a second, but Elizabeth recognized it was Sarah, the flight attendant she had met en route to Scotland. She wore a full face of makeup and an unzipped black jacket over a blouse, very different from her work uniform that Elizabeth had grown accustomed to.

"Woah, you're here! It's Sarah, right?" Elizabeth asked. Her friends seemed confused.

"Who's this?" Alexa wedged herself between the two of them.

"This is Sarah, one of the flight attendants I met on the plane."

"It's nice to meet you." Sarah offered her hand, and Alexa shook it.

"You too. I'm Alexa, Elizabeth's coworker."

"And this is Brooke and Marcus," Elizabeth said. The two of them waved to Sarah.

"Five shots," the bartender said with a thick Scottish accent that caught Elizabeth by surprise, and Sarah handed over her credit card. The five of them grabbed their drinks.

"To new friends," Alexa said, staring intently at Sarah. Elizabeth wasn't sure, but she thought Alexa was blushing.

"Cheers!" They yelled, clinking their glasses together and throwing back their shots.

For the second time tonight, Elizabeth regretted forgetting the chaser as she felt the drink slip down her throat, burning every inch of her esophagus until it reached the pit of her stomach.

"Come on, let me introduce you to *my* friends." Sarah added the bartender's tip, signed the receipt, and tossed her credit card in the tiny purse that hung from her elbow.

"There's more of you?" Alexa asked.

"Of course not. There's only one of me." Sarah winked, grabbed Alexa's hand, and dragged her toward a booth where three more people sat.

Alexa looked back at Elizabeth and motioned for her to follow. As she walked up, she recognized them as the other flight attendants from her plane—the older woman, a younger woman, and a man that looked similar in age to Elizabeth. The man was the only one still dressed in his work uniform. Sarah crawled into the booth beside the older woman and pulled Alexa beside her.

"Who are your friends?" The man asked.

"This is Alexa," Sarah said, placing her hand on Alexa's shoulder, "and this is Elizabeth. I met her on the flight. These are her friends, Brooke and Marcus, right?"

"That's right," Marcus said, moving two chairs from the high-top tables to the booth for Brooke, Elizabeth, and himself.

"These are my coworkers: Christine," she pointed across the table to the younger girl, "Chuck," she motioned her hand to the guy sitting next to Christine, "and Kelly."

"It's nice to meet you all," Alexa said while the rest exchanged smiles and waves.

"So, what brings you guys to Scotland?" Chuck asked. His eyes were on Alexa, but Marcus was the one to answer.

"They're here for work, but we just tagged along for the vacay."

"Work, huh? What do you do?" Chuck asked, his eyes still on Alexa.

"We're marine biologists," Elizabeth said.

"They're studying turtles," Sarah said. Alexa seemed surprised that she already knew that.

"Turtles?" Kelly set her coffee mug down. "What's so exciting about them?"

"Well, they're sea turtles, to be exact," Elizabeth explained.

"I wouldn't say it's exciting, but we are trying to figure out what they're doing in Loch Ness instead of the sea," Alexa said.

"Are you guys doing okay over here?" asked the waiter as he approached the table carrying an empty black server tray.

"Can we get some more drinks?" Sarah asked.

"What would you like?"

"A vodka cranberry ... right?" Sarah looked at Elizabeth.

"Wow, you remembered. Yeah, I'd love one of those."

"I'll take a sex on the beach, and what do you guys drink?" Sarah turned to Alexa and placed her hand on her shoulder.

"That sounds great," Alexa said, smiling. "But I think I'll just take a shot of vodka."

"A rum and coke," Marcus said.

"A tequila sunrise, please!" Brooke exclaimed.

"A little bit of everything. I got you. I'll be right back." The waiter headed for the bar.

"So, do you already have a theory on why the turtles are here?" Christine asked. She had been so silent to this point Elizabeth had forgotten she was even there.

"Not really. We have a few preliminary thoughts, but we won't know until we see them out there."

"But enough about us," Brooke said, "I would like to hear more about *your* job. Flight attendant. That sounds awesome! Getting to see the world has always been a dream of mine."

"Dream? More like a nightmare. At least when you've been doing it for over forty years," Kelly stated.

"It can't be *that* bad," Marcus said.

"It wasn't always, but after the first few years, it just keeps getting worse. You start to hate half of the places you go. The weather constantly fluctuates from one extreme to another, airplane passengers treat you like shit, you never know what currency to bring, and you never know what to order off the menus. At this point in my life, I just want the simple things. Rest and relaxation."

"I've got those drinks for you," the waiter said as he passed them out, remembering who ordered what.

"Thanks," Marcus said when the waiter was walking away.

"Well, unlike Kelly, I enjoy getting out of the States. Being away from my life and kid at home feels so freeing. I can be whoever I want, and nobody relevant to me will know about it. I feel like I can get into all kinds of trouble," Sarah said, picking up her glass and placing her free hand on Alexa's thigh.

Alexa's eyes widened, and Elizabeth was sure she was blushing this time. Perhaps it was the alcohol.

"Legal trouble only, of course. I wouldn't want to end up in a foreign jail. That wouldn't be freeing now, would it?" Sarah tightened her grip on Alexa's thigh while she took a sip.

Alexa picked up her glass and gulped down the vodka. Unable to handle the shot, she skeeved out, shook her head, and leaned backward over the booth with a full-face cringe.

Elizabeth caught Sarah staring at Alexa's nipples, poking through her tank top.

"Aren't you cold in that outfit?" Sarah asked.

"Not after *that*," Alexa pointed to her glass on the table as if it had committed a crime. "I think I need another one."

"Why don't you just get something to sip on?" Elizabeth suggested. "If we stay here for a while, you don't want to get blackout drunk in the first hour."

"Nope, I need another. Waiter!" Alexa raised her hand and called him over.

Over the next few hours, the group got well acquainted. Elizabeth shared stories about how their clique met, she talked with Sarah about Hailey, and Sarah mentioned her son, who was around the same age and at home with his father. She made it very clear they were separated and that, except for the birth of her son, she regretted having sex with him. Elizabeth related all too well to that statement.

At some point in their conversation, between Brooke giving Marcus a death stare for gawking at Alexa's chest and Kelly's story about her first trip to Amsterdam, Alexa had made a joke about Chuck looking like a male stripper in his flight attendant uniform. From then on, Chuck had an apparent and serious infatuation with her. While that wasn't surprising, Elizabeth was shocked at Alexa's more-than-friendly flirting with Sarah. Alexa was always promiscuous, and Elizabeth had front-row seats to all the men she would take home in college, but there had never been any women in those ventures. This was new.

Chapter 5

I Kissed a Girl

"I think they're kicking us out of here," Marcus said as the overhead lights reached maximum brightness. The remaining patrons exited the pub, and the staff started wiping down the tables.

"Yeah, we should probably get out of here," Chuck agreed.

"Aw, so soon?" Sarah sighed. "I could stay here all night."

"I know, right? I was having so much fun," Alexa said.

"Stay any longer, and you'll get locked in here," Brooke slurred.

"That won't be so bad," Sarah said, "but let me grab my purse." She turned to her right and leaned over Kelly, who had fallen asleep, to grab her purse wedged between Kelly and the wall. "Kelly, time to wake up."

"What?" Kelly opened her eyes. "Are we finally leaving?"

"Unfortunately," Sarah said.

"Thank God. A woman my age needs her beauty sleep." Kelly grabbed her things and exited the booth. They all followed Marcus and Brooke to the exit.

"Thank you for coming," the waiter said. "You guys are coming back before you leave the country, right?"

"It's not likely for us. We have to work the next flight home tomorrow," Chuck said.

"*We* will *definitely* be back," Brooke promised, stumbling over her feet while exiting the building.

"Wait, you guys are already leaving?" Alexa turned and asked Sarah while they stood behind the exit door.

"I know, it sucks. I hoped we could hang out more," Sarah grazed Alexa's arm.

"Hello!" A Scottish man called from behind them, scaring Alexa.

He approached the group and handed them all business cards. The card's front side featured a stunning shot of Loch Ness with the title "Corey's Boats and Tours" at the top.

"What's this?" Elizabeth asked.

"This is my business. We offer cruises, smaller boat rentals, and tour packages as well. Anything you need," he said. His breath reeked of alcohol.

"Are you Corey?" Elizabeth asked.

"I am," he smiled.

"Thanks, dude, but I think we'll be okay," Alexa said, turning away from the man and walking toward the parking lot with the rest of the group. Then the man grabbed Sarah by the arm and she squealed, yanking it away.

"Don't fucking touch me," Sarah said.

"What the fuck is wrong with you?" Alexa asked.

"Wait, wait. Please. I'll give you guys a discount if you come by in the next three days," Corey said.

"She said no, you creep!" Alexa grabbed Sarah and stood in front of her.

"Walk away, man," Marcus said.

"No, I'm sorry—"

"Walk away," Alexa said, her face fuming with anger.

"Fuck you. Fucking Americans ..." Corey walked away, muttering under his breath.

"Are you okay?" Alexa turned back to Sarah.

"Yeah, I'll be fine. He just grabbed my arm. What the fuck was his problem?" The group stared Corey down while he stumbled through the parking lot, got in his car, and drove away.

"That can't be the best way to advertise a business," Elizabeth said as she analyzed the card in her hand. "I'd rather take one of my uncle's cruises, anyway."

"I am *exhausted*. Can we hurry and get out of here?" Brooke pleaded.

"Yeah, I'm pretty tired too. And I still have to drive," Marcus said.

"Really? I was hoping we would hang out a little longer," Sarah said. Her fellow flight attendants looked at her like she had just pissed on their shoes.

"No way, I am going home and getting right into bed," Kelly said.

"Yeah, I'm with Kelly on this one," Christine nodded.

"I don't think it's a great idea. I was hoping to get up early tomorrow to take Hailey shopping around town," Elizabeth said.

Sarah looked at Alexa like a begging puppy. Alexa had been tiptoeing around her interest in Sarah all night. She had never felt interested in another woman before, and she wasn't sure why she was feeling this way now, but she knew that this girl in front of her made her feel something that no man had before. And she wanted more. Now, she faced the difficult decision between pursuing this newfound interest or going home and pretending like it never happened.

What would my friends think? What about my parents? What if the night was amazing, but I never saw her again?

She chose to go with what felt right at the time. "I'll stay a while longer if you will," She grabbed Sarah's hand while she spoke.

"You will?" Marcus asked, raising one eyebrow in confusion and then the other, once he realized what was happening between them.

"How will you get home?" Elizabeth asked.

"I'll get her a taxi," Sarah said.

"Just leave the door open for me," Alexa said.

"Let's just go! I'm too tired for this right now," Brooke tugged at Marcus's arm.

"Just ... be safe," Elizabeth said.

Alexa thought about the creepy guy, Corey, but she felt safe since they watched him leave.

"She'll be fine, I promise," Sarah assured them.

"I won't bolt the hotel door. You have a key, right?" Christine asked.

"Yep, go on. I'll see you in the morning," Sarah said.

Alexa and Sarah watched as their friends walked to their separate rental cars and drove away.

"Alright, the party-poopers are gone. Why don't we take this down to the beach?" Sarah asked.

Alexa looked across the street at the steep decline toward the loch, and at this point, she was willing to try whatever this girl wanted. "That sounds great."

They crossed the street, gazed down the small hill, and found an opening in the shrubbery that appeared to be a small pathway made by people walking through. "So, I have to ask...." Alexa stepped carefully down the hill. "And please forgive me if I'm wrong." She offered her hand to Sarah and helped her climb down behind her.

"What is it?" Sarah took her last step down the hill, and they started following the path.

"Have I been completely misreading signals this whole time, or were you coming on to me all night?"

Sarah giggled and grabbed Alexa's hand, clasping her fingers between hers. "Why else would I be walking down this dark, mysterious, hidden pathway in the middle of the night with you?"

"I don't know. You could be a serial killer, for all I know."

Sarah burst into laughter. "Yeah, that's my story. I'm a flight attendant by day and a serial killer by night."

"Hey, it's not like you have to try too hard to leave the country after you claim your victims." Alexa felt a cold chill blow in, making her realize how much colder she should feel, but she had the alcohol to thank for keeping her warm. She also had to thank it for the confidence it gave her to be with Sarah here and now.

Sarah giggled and leaned closely to Alexa, resting her head on her shoulder while they walked.

"So I guess that means I properly read the signals, right?" Alexa asked.

Sarah tilted her head upward to meet eyes with Alexa. "Yeah, you did."

Alexa wrapped her arm around her. "I thought so, but I was worried when you mentioned having a kid."

"What, because I had a kid, you thought I wasn't into girls?"

"Well, yeah."

"Not everything in life has to be so black and white. I enjoy *people*, especially those I can have fun with. Man or woman. If they are up for a good time, I'm willing to have it with them."

"That ... sounds like a great outlook on life." Alexa looked up to the moon. "So, how is it?"

"What?"

"Raising a kid. I see Elizabeth raising her daughter, and while she is such a smart and well-behaved girl, I just know how crazy she drives her mom."

"It is the most demanding, stressful job you could ever ask for, but it is also the most rewarding. I love my son more than anything, but he drives me crazy too."

The path brought them to a small, concave-shaped opening in the surrounding shrubbery where the loch met land. The ground beneath them was a black pebble beach.

"Tonight is gonna be a perfect one, isn't it?" Sarah asked.

"That's what it feels like. Just ... before we go any further, I wanted to say that I've never felt like this with a girl before. This whole thing is new to me."

"I thought so. Don't even think about it. Just answer this, do you want to have some fun?"

Yes, Alexa thought. "Of course I do, I just—" Alexa's sentence was cut short when Sarah's mouth met hers, and any questions she had about her new feelings were answered. They collapsed to the ground, Alexa's ass landed hard on the pebbles, and they laughed.

Whatever this was between her and Sarah, Alexa liked it. She liked how soft Sarah's hands felt when they entered the back of her shirt and scratched her back. She liked how the warmth of her tongue further distracted her from how cold it was here by the water. She liked the smell of her perfume. She liked the unhindered, passionate energy she radiated when she climbed on top of her. She liked feeling like she was getting away with something. But most of all, she liked how natural it felt.

She wasn't sure if this feeling was something that she had been hiding from all these years, or if this was something that she was searching for with all of the men that she had crawled into bed with, or if this was a feeling that she wasn't meant to experience until she met Sarah. Whatever the case may be, she was here now, and she was ready to give in to all of her emotions.

Sarah leaned away just long enough to peel off her jacket and unbutton her blouse; then, she returned for more. "I have—" she ripped open her shirt and reached down to unbutton her pants, "a fun idea."

"Oh, *God*." Alexa started unbuttoning her pants.

Sarah peeled off her blouse and threw it to the side, then she unhooked her bra and let it slide down her arm, falling onto Alexa's face. Her breasts stared at Alexa like a pair of eyes, and Alexa stared back like a deer in headlights. She had seen plenty of tits in her life, even had a pair of her own, but this was the first time she was excited to see them, aside from the fact that she didn't even know what to do with them.

Alexa hurried to kick off her shoes, slip off her pants, and reach her hand to grope Sarah's right breast, but Sarah stood up before she could.

"I think we should go swimming," Sarah said.

That was her idea? Alexa thought. Sarah stepped out of her shoes and, in one fell swoop, pulled her pants and panties down to her ankles, removing one foot from them at a time.

"What, you mean skinny dip?" Alexa asked.

"Unless you want me to put my clothes back on."

"I didn't say that ... but this water has gotta be *freezing*."

"Then we will use each other's bodies to keep warm," Sarah walked to the water and dipped a toe in first, then stepped in and entered the loch until she was ankle-deep. "Aren't you coming?"

Alexa was envious of the confidence that she radiated through her naked body. Sarah didn't have the supermodel body type that Alexa had always strived for, but she admired it as a work of art. "I think I'm good here. I like the view." A cold breeze blew in, and Alexa's eyes grew tired, reminding her she was still drunk.

Sarah stepped deeper into the water. "If you're not gonna come in, why did you take your pants off?" Sarah asked, and Alexa kept quiet. "Oh, you thought we were gonna—" Sarah smiled. "On the first date? You're naughty." She held out her index finger and waved it left and right to shame Alexa.

"So, that's what this is? A date?"

"If you don't make it weird. Now, are you gonna sit over there all night, or will you take your clothes off and come get me?"

Alexa was tired, drunk, and cold, but she wanted this. She stood up and removed her socks first, then her jeans, cardigan, and finally her tank top, which Sarah applauded.

"I don't know about this," Alexa said, cupping her naked breasts. She could feel the goosebumps against her palms.

"Panties. Off." Sarah pointed at them.

"Geez, you're so demanding," Alexa joked, but she obliged, peeled them down to the ground, then threw them on top of her pile of clothes.

"How else would I get you out of your clothes?"

"You could've taken them off yourself."

"But telling you to do it felt so much better."

Alexa held her arms over her chest to keep warm and stepped into the water. It was ice cold.

"What the *fuck*? It's freezing!"

"Just get in and get it over with. Don't make me beg," Sarah said.

"Fine."

Alexa held her breath and stepped into the loch—doing her best not to think about it— and kept going deeper and deeper, letting the freezing water consume her body one inch at a time, until it was just her head that remained above the surface beside Sarah. When she finally exhaled, she saw her breath turn to frost in the air.

"I'm in now, happy?" Alexa asked and pulled Sarah to her, hugging her tightly. Her skin felt like ecstasy against her own—soft, warm, and comforting.

"So happy." Sarah kissed her once and pulled away, backstroking gracefully across the water.

Alexa thought she looked like the mermaid she always wanted to be as a kid, only more pretty than she ever could've imagined.

"Chase me," Sarah said.

"What—" Alexa was caught off guard when Sarah splashed her with a kick from her foot, covering her face with water.

Sarah turned to her stomach and swam away. She was fast, but Alexa was determined to catch up to her. She didn't know what she would do when she caught her, but whatever game this was, she was enjoying it. She felt alive.

Alexa swam as hard as she could, losing sight of Sarah between the splashes of water from her strokes, but she knew the general direction that she was going. It was when she looked up to check the distance between the two of them that she noticed she was gone. At first, she thought Sarah had hidden underwater as a prank or another game where she would pop out from underneath and scare her, but she never surfaced.

"Sarah?" Alexa called out, but the air was silent aside from the sound of the small waves of the loch and the crickets in the shrubbery surrounding her. Alexa added terror to the list of mixed feelings she was having throughout the night, and if that wasn't bad enough, she started to feel sick to her stomach.

Alexa turned back to the beach, hoping Sarah would be there, but she wasn't. Her mouth began to salivate. She rushed to shore as fast as she could and vomited profusely into the first bush she approached. Whenever she felt like the puking was over, more would come. She felt short of breath, first from the swimming and now from insufficient time to breathe between upchucking. Her knees felt weak, and she was starting to get dizzy.

She fell to the ground, the damp pebbles cold as they scraped her ass. Her blinking grew heavier once she laid her head on the floor.

"Sarah." Her voice was weak as she used the last of her energy to call her name one final time before her eyes wouldn't open anymore tonight.

Chapter 6

Meet the Family

The drive back to Castle Bradley was dark and silent. Brooke fell asleep as soon as her butt touched the car seat, and Marcus used all of his remaining energy to focus on the road. Elizabeth stared at Loch Ness the whole way home, only averting her gaze now and then to make sure Marcus wasn't nodding off.

When they arrived, they found that Monica had left the gate open for them and the porch light on. As instructed, Marcus drove to the right side of the house and found a driveway surrounding what looked like an eight-car garage. A silver Honda Civic was parked carelessly in the middle of the driveway, likely by Monica, and Marcus parked as carelessly as she did. He turned the car off and jostled Brooke's shoulder until she opened her eyes.

"Come on, let's get to bed," he said, and she didn't argue. Brooke radiated energy like the short nap gave her a whole night's rest. She clung tightly to Marcus's arm as they trudged around the house to the front door, where he used Monica's key. The lock clicked open, and they stepped inside. The foyer was illuminated only by wall candles, and the house was otherwise dark. They left their shoes at the door, and Elizabeth led the way down the dark hallway, using her phone's screensaver as their only light source. "I'll see you in the morning," she said when Brooke and Marcus entered their room. She heard their door lock behind her as soon as it shut. When Elizabeth approached her bedroom door, she noticed the light from the gap beneath i t.

Monica better not have let Hailey stay awake this late! Elizabeth double-checked the time on her phone, and it read 2:57 a. m. She opened the door slowly to avoid making too much noise, but it creaked open like she always imagined an old castle's doors would. When she entered the room, she gasped upon realizing it was empty. The blankets on Hailey's bed were thrown to the side like she had gotten out of bed. "Hailey?" She called, but there was no response. She stepped into the bathroom and flicked on the light switch. Empty.

Where could she be?

Elizabeth ran out of the bedroom and through the elongated hallway, furiously knocking on Monica's door once she got to it.

"Elizabeth?" A voice called from behind her.

"Fuck!" Elizabeth jumped at the sound of it, her heart racing.

Monica stood there, wearing a soft-pink nightgown that hung just below her thighs. She reached over and flicked a light switch on the wall, brightening the hallway. In her hands, smoke rose from a white coffee mug containing a dark liquid. "What's the matter? You look like you've seen a ghost!"

"Where's Hailey?" Elizabeth asked.

"She's in bed," she took a sip from her mug, "She came to my door not long ago saying she couldn't sleep, so I made her some herbal tea and tucked her in. I was having the same problem and made myself some too." She held up the mug.

"Well, she's not there anymore."

"Are you sure?"

"Yes, I'm sure. I just checked! That room is empty."

"Oh, that's not good. Come on, let's look for her. She couldn't have gotten far." Monica offered her hand to lead her through the house, but Elizabeth wasn't sure.

"We should probably split up. This house is pretty big. We could find her faster that way."

"You're probably right. Have your friends gone to bed yet?"

"We could check—" Elizabeth stopped once she heard Brooke moan through the door. "Never mind. Let's just find her."

Elizabeth split from Monica as soon as they left the hallway. Monica searched the bottom floor while Elizabeth brought her attention to the stairs.

If I knew my daughter, that's exactly where she'd go.

Elizabeth crept up the stairs, her hand sliding across the freshly polished banister. Her socks slipped on the carpeted staircase with every step, her balance off from a night of drinking, but she managed to reach the top still on her feet.

The upper level was eerily silent as she made her way through the various halls, calling Hailey's name every so often as she checked every room, door to door. As she neared what she thought was the last room, she started to worry. She was getting ready to check if Monica had found her yet, and resort to calling the police if she hadn't.

This is the last room. It must be Bradley's, she thought. The door was cracked open and the light was on. Elizabeth approached the door and heard a tired man's voice from inside.

"She ... She was a wonderful woman." The man coughed. "Your grandfather too. He was a lot of fun. The life of the party type."

He must be talking to Hailey!

"It's a shame your mother never told you about them, but I understand. I mean, look at *me.* What your mother and I went through ... I wouldn't want to relive that. And your mother was so young at the time. You remind me of her."

"What was it like? That night?" Hailey said.

Thank God she's okay.

"Petrifying. I remember being unable to move, forced to sit there and watch my entire life, everything I've ever known, taken away from me. The sounds of screams ... the bodies. Wanting to help, but my legs refusing to do anything but quiver."

Elizabeth remembered it all too well. Petrifying was a great way to describe it. Hearing him talk about it now brought that feeling right back to her. She felt her hair stand up on her arms, sweat forming in her armpits and along her back. She never told Hailey about what happened because she never could. She contemplated stopping Bradley from telling her about it, but if *he* didn't explain to her why she didn't have a real family, then nobody ever would.

"And worst of all," Bradley said, "the monster."

Wait, what?

"Monster?" Hailey asked.

"That's right, the monster," Bradley said. "We were swimming for our lives, your mother and me. I'll never forget the look in its eyes. It wasn't even aware of the pain it caused, ripping our entire family apart, limb to limb. It was just hungry. Or maybe it was just having fun, hunting us for sport—" Elizabeth interrupted, pushing his door open and lifting Hailey from the floor.

It disturbed Elizabeth how amused Hailey looked instead of terrified, but she would have to deal with that later.

Bradley looked sickly lying in a hospital bed: IV drip in one arm, his face disfigured and hardly recognizable to her, and a leg missing under the thin blanket with a plethora of tubes and wires running beneath it.

"What's the matter with you? Telling a child a silly story like that?" Elizabeth scolded.

"Wow ... you've really grown." Bradley coughed into his hand. "Now, I have hundreds of words I've used to describe that night, and silly is *not* one of them."

"Mommy, it's okay—" Hailey tried to speak, but Elizabeth interrupted.

"I'm sorry, baby, but it's not," Elizabeth said.

"Is everything okay?" Monica asked from the hallway behind Elizabeth. She spotted Hailey in her arms. "Oh my gosh! Did she wake you up, Bradley? I'm sorry, I was supposed to watch her."

Bradley waved her off like it was no problem.

"It's not your fault, Monica. Hailey is big enough to know when she should be in bed." Elizabeth put her down and gave

Hailey's hand to Monica. "Can you take her back to bed, please? I need to have a word with my cousin."

"But Mommy—" Hailey tried to speak again.

"But nothing. Go to bed now. You should've been sleeping for hours, and you know it."

Hailey dropped her head low and walked into the hallway with Monica.

"Thank you," Elizabeth said and closed the door behind them.

"Elizabeth," Bradley spoke calmly.

Elizabeth felt her heart race like it did when she was on the yacht. She started pacing back and forth along the room's perimeter, scratching at her arms.

"Lizzy!" Bradley raised his voice, and she stopped pacing beside the window in the room, this one located similarly to the window in her room downstairs, only slightly larger and with a telescope pointing through it and a rifle displayed above it.

"I haven't been called that since the accident."

"I'm not surprised. You never really liked it. You would always call it 'unprofessional,' but we were your family, and we didn't care."

"I still don't like it."

"And I still don't care."

"As far as I'm concerned, that version of me died that night."

"You're drunk."

"You think *that's* the problem here? You just don't get it, do you?"

"I didn't say that it was the problem. I'm just saying that you might be overreacting."

"How *dare* you tell me I'm overreacting! Our whole family was full of fucking drunks, and you were no exception! What happened to our family that night was awful, but even that could never mask the memory of you pulling your dick out in front of me and pissing off the side of the boat! Since you have so much to say tonight, why don't you say something about *that?*" Elizabeth stared at him, her eyes red with hatred. "Have you ever had a grown man splash his piss onto your face?" She waited for an answer, knowing one wasn't coming. He looked embarrassed and ashamed of himself. "I didn't think so. I was a *child*! That is just *so* disgusting. It is no wonder that I fell down the alcoholic rabbit hole after what the fuck I've gone through. That night on the boat took everything from me, not just my family. All of my hopes and dreams died that night too. I lived every day with nightmares, rewatching the horrors of the people I love screaming and dying in front of me. And to tell my daughter that was all the work of some fucking monster—"

"I'm sorry!" He yelled and sat up straight in bed. "I can't speak for my actions back then. I have spent every day working on becoming a better man, and I would like to think that I'm a different person than I used to be. I know that I'm not, but I'm trying. Maybe I overstepped with Hailey, but I knew your parents, and they would like their granddaughter to hear about them. And *you* shouldn't pretend like they didn't exist. They raised you, and they deserve to live on in our memories. I know it's hard. I lost just as many people that night as you."

"Sure you did, but I'd say you came out of that night much better than I did. You got to live lavishly in a castle and have a pretty young girl take care of you. I had to go from foster home to foster home, suffering daily until I worked hard enough to earn better."

"All the money in the world couldn't replace what we lost that night, and you know that. But they were real and deserve to live on in our thoughts."

Elizabeth analyzed all of the machines keeping his poor, frail body alive and felt a bit of regret at her words.

Maybe his life hasn't been better than hers.

"I just ... I was lost when I had Hailey. I had nothing and wanted nothing. I don't ever want her to experience that."

"I know. You're a good mom, much like your own mother."

"I'm sorry." Tears filled her eyes.

"Don't be. I know I wasn't a great cousin to you. I should've reached out earlier. I should've sent you money to help you get by. I just ... assumed you wouldn't want anything to do with me. What I did was disgusting, and yet another regret on my list. I miss our family so much; you two are all I have left. I don't want to lose you, too."

Maybe he really has grown up. Elizabeth felt sorry for him. He had Monica, but he was alone. Elizabeth was fortunate enough to start her own family with Hailey, but Bradley didn't have the same luck.

Elizabeth rubbed her hand on the telescope, looking out the window to change the subject. "Do you spend a lot of time looking through here?"

"Every day."

"How could you? I feel uneasy just being close to the damn loch, but seeing it every day ... I couldn't imagine."

"Then why did you come back?"

"I told you on the phone. I'm studying the turtles in the loch."

"I know what you said on the phone, but I want to know the true reason. There are plenty of turtles all over the world and plenty of other aquatic unknowns out there. Why did you insist on coming back to Loch Ness?"

"Because I want to know what happened that night," Elizabeth said. It was the first time she had spoken the reason for coming here out loud, and now it felt real.

"Exactly," Bradley said.

"What do you mean?"

"I look out that window every night for the same reason. I'm searching for answers day in and day out, but I've found none."

"Still, telling my daughter some crazy story about a monster is just ... wrong. This isn't some usual boogeyman story you tell a kid to scare them. It's something that actually happened that Hailey has been looking for answers for her whole life."

"It's not just some crazy story. The monster is real."

Elizabeth looked back at him like he was dumb. "What the *fuck* are you talking about?"

"I saw it. That night."

"No, you didn't."

"I did. What do you think pulled me away when we were swimming?"

"The tide."

"No. It was a monster. I looked that thing in the eye before it sunk its teeth into my leg and pulled me under."

"You must've imagined it. I'm sure you lost a lot of blood during the accident."

"Yeah, because it bit my fucking leg off."

"It just doesn't make any sense."

"It doesn't have to. But it happened."

"It was probably another turtle. Just like the one that saved me!"

"This thing was huge."

"Sea turtles are big."

"I didn't say big. I said huge. It was like the size of the yacht, if not bigger."

"No, there's no way. If something like that existed, the public would've seen it by now."

"I saw it."

"I mean, hundreds of people. The loch isn't deep enough to keep something that large hidden."

"I'm not the biologist here, but I don't think that's entirely true, and I don't think you do either."

"What *do* you think?"

"I think you wouldn't have come out here without a theory. I'm not sure what that is, but it gives me hope. You don't have to tell me what that is, but I hope you find it."

He was right, but Elizabeth didn't want to say. She *did* have a theory, but she was hoping she was wrong. Having your family die in a tragic accident sounds better than death by Loch Ness Monster.

"Have you seen anything out there?" Elizabeth pressed her left eye against the telescope lens and watched the still water.

"Never. Which frustrates me."

"That would frustrate me too." She backed away from the telescope and glanced at the rifle hanging on a plaque above the window. It was massive, like one big game hunters would use to bring down larger animals like elephants. "What's that for?"

"I told you I've been looking out that window for answers. That rifle is for when I find them."

She thought about what she would do if she found her answers. What if there was a monster down there? Would she be driven to kill it or study it?

"Lizzy."

She turned and looked at him.

He held a clear glass with melting ice cubes inside. "Can we just start over? I'm sorry ... about everything. I want us, no, I *need* us to be okay with each other."

"Okay, just please don't fill Hailey's head with any more unproven monster stories," Elizabeth said.

Bradley smiled and swirled the ice around in his glass. "I would like to get to know her. She is so bright and innocent. I need a lot more of that around here."

Elizabeth laughed. "Of course! She is the happiest girl in the world. I don't know where I'd be without her."

"And she is just *so* smart for her age."

"She really is."

"She reminds me of you, you know. Before everything. I can tell you've done a great job raising her."

Elizabeth smiled.

Bradley opened the drawer in his nightstand, pulled out a metal flask, and poured it into his glass. "Old habits die hard. At least now I don't drink to get stupid; I drink just enough to numb the pain and go to sleep."

Elizabeth laughed, "I understand that. I've been there plenty of times. Only my pain was emotional. What are you drinking?"

"Bourbon."

Elizabeth cringed, "Yeah, that would put me to sleep too." She walked to the door. "Well, I'm gonna head to bed and apologize to Hailey. I'll see you tomorrow."

"Good night."

"Get some sleep."

Bradley pulled the string on the lamp on his nightstand, and the light went out. Elizabeth shut the door behind her as she exited and headed down the hall and the stairs.

Monica sat on a couch, waiting for her in the foyer. She stood up when she saw Elizabeth. "I am so sorry."

"Don't worry about it."

"I should've been watching her. I am so, so sorry."

"Hey, it's okay. She just wanted to meet another member of our family. The *only* other member. I can't be mad that she was curious."

"Okay, I just feel terrible. I thought she was completely lost. But I tucked her back in. She kept insisting that she wasn't tired, but I could see it in her eyes that she was."

"She's always been defiant, but you have nothing to worry about. I'll see you in the morning."

"Of course."

Elizabeth started for the hallway but stopped briefly before she continued. "Hey, did Alexa ever make it home?"

Monica appeared confused. "Didn't she come home with you?"

"No, she ... found someone."

"Oh, she works quickly. I didn't think she would find a guy out here that fast."

"It wasn't a guy."

"Oh! Is she a lesbian? I had no idea!"

"Yeah, neither did we. I don't think she did either."

Monica looked lost for words.

"Trust me. We were all just as surprised."

"Okay, well, I'll keep the door unlocked for her."

"Thank you." Elizabeth continued down the hall and to her bedroom.

Hailey lay in bed, pretending to sleep, but Elizabeth could tell her eyes were half open.

"Hey, baby."

Hailey pretended to snore. Elizabeth tickled her stomach, and she smiled before bursting into full laughter.

"There she is! I just wanted to apologize. I shouldn't have freaked out like that. I'm glad you got to meet Bradley."

"He's really nice."

"I'm glad. Now, you get some rest, okay? I'm just going to get dressed for bed. Then I'll go to sleep too."

"But what about the monster?" Hailey asked.

"If there's a monster out there, I will find it. But it's nothing to worry about, okay?"

"Okay."

"Now get some rest. I love you."

"I love you too." Hailey closed her eyes.

Elizabeth kissed Hailey's forehead. "Good night." She waited for her to say it back, but Hailey had already fallen asleep.

Chapter 7

The Morning After

If the piercing headache wasn't a convincing enough reason to wake up, the sudden urge to vomit sure was. Elizabeth threw the pile of blankets off the bed in an uncoordinated but quick fashion. She hopped off the bed and tried to rush to the bathroom, but her foot got caught in the tangled mess of blankets she had just created. Slipping forehead first into the bathroom's door frame, she was left with a small bruise that would surely swell later, but that was the least of her concerns. She untangled her bare foot and crawled the rest of the way, barely fast enough to reach the toilet before the contents of her stomach forced their way out her mouth and splashed water in her face.

The sound of footsteps approached from the bedroom.

"Hailey, don't come in here!" She yelled and waved her hand back to signal her away.

"It's not Hailey. It's me, Monica."

Elizabeth rested her head on the toilet seat to see the doorway where Monica tiptoed around the corner and into the bathroom.

"Are you okay?" Monica said, worried and rushing to her side. She gathered Elizabeth's hair and pulled a hair tie from her wrist to put it into a messy ponytail, just in time for Elizabeth to hurl some more.

"Where's Hailey?" Elizabeth spat what remained in her mouth.

"She's okay. She's in the bar with Bradley and your friends."

"Okay, good. I hate it when she sees me like this." Elizabeth sat up and crawled away from the toilet, resting her back against the bathroom wall. "Did you say Bradley? He came downstairs?"

"Yes, he was in a good mood after last night. It sounds like the two of you had some sort of misunderstanding but are okay now, right?"

"That about sums it up." Elizabeth stood tall and flushed the toilet. "I'm sorry if I was rude last night. I was perhaps a little too tipsy."

"Don't worry about it."

"Excuse me." Elizabeth stepped to the sink and washed her hands and face.

"I'll let them know you're awake."

"Thank you. I'm going to shower then meet you guys in the bar."

"Of course." Monica exited the room.

Elizabeth returned to the bedroom to dig through her bags for her travel toothbrush and went back into the bathroom to brush her teeth. She scrubbed her tongue furiously and spat, then washed the remaining toothpaste off her lips.

She returned to the bedroom and wheeled her luggage into the bathroom but was too lazy to pick out her outfit. She removed her clothes, opened the glass shower door, and entered the square, freestanding shower. The shower head spilled ice-cold water over her naked body while she fiddled with the handles. Once the temperature felt right, she leaned against the cold tile wall and slid to the floor.

O nce Elizabeth was dressed and ready for the day, she met her friends in the castle bar.

"There she is!" Brooke sat loosely on her bar stool.

"Good morning!" Hailey yelled from the floor, where she sat with a coloring book.

"Good morning, baby," Elizabeth said.

"We were just getting to know Bradley; he seems like he must've been a fun uncle," Marcus said from his seat beside Brooke's.

"Well, Lizzy didn't think so ... but I can't blame her," Bradley said. He sat in a wheelchair against the wall to the bar's left, where Monica poured them drinks.

"Lizzy?" Marcus laughed, and Brooke appeared frustrated.

"You never let us call you that!" Brooke shouted.

"And for good reason," Elizabeth said.

Monica handed Bradley his glass, filled with orange juice and vodka: a proper breakfast beverage. "Can I make you something?" Monica asked.

"No thanks, it's too early for me." Elizabeth sat beside Marcus.

"Are you sure? It might help with that hangover."

"I'll be okay. That shower was life-changing. But speaking of hangovers, where's Alexa?"

"She never came out of her room," Marcus said.

"Are you sure she was even in there?"

"What, she didn't come home last night?" Brooke asked.

"I'll go check." Marcus got up from his stool and headed for the hall.

"What's up with her, anyway? I know I wasn't the only one picking up serious lesbian vibes from her last night." Brooke spun around on her stool like a bored child.

"Yeah, I'm not sure," Elizabeth said.

"I mean, if she is a lesbian, that's fine. I just never saw her act that way before," Brooke continued.

"Yeah, me neither."

"Come to think of it, she's seen me naked so many times! Well, topless, at least. Was she staring at us the whole time?"

"I don't know; why don't you ask her?"

"Because that would be insensitive!"

"Exactly. So stop worrying about it. Whatever happened last night was new. You would've noticed her flirting if she had been into you this whole time. It's not like she ever hides it."

"She doesn't have to flirt to stare."

Elizabeth rolled her eyes.

"I'm sorry. What exactly happened last night?" Bradley asked.

"Long story—" Elizabeth stopped as Marcus yelled.

"She's not here!" He ran into the bar. "She's not in her room *or* the bathroom. I don't think she came home."

"Fuck, really?" Brooke asked.

"She doesn't even have a phone. We have to go look for her," Elizabeth said.

"I knew it was a bad idea last night," Brooke said. "We don't even know where she is."

"We have to go back to the pub. It's the only place we can check," Marcus said.

Elizabeth turned to Monica. "I hate to ask, but I have to go with them. Can you please watch Hailey again?"

"Yes, of course! Go, find her!" Monica said.

Elizabeth knelt on the floor beside Hailey. "Hey, baby. Would you like to hang out with Monica and Bradley today?"

"You're leaving again?" Hailey asked.

"I have to. Alexa might be in trouble, and we need to go find her."

"Is she going to be okay?"

"I'm sure she will be *just* fine. But Mommy has to help her. You can help by being good and listening to Monica, okay?"

Hailey nodded in agreement.

Elizabeth stood tall and brushed off her jeans. "Let's go."

Alexa woke to the sound of something splashing in the water. *Last night must've been a dream, and a weird one at that,* she thought. She opened her eyes. A small wave rode up the beach and grazed her feet, the coolness of the water being the only positive sensation her body felt.

Wait, water? She fought through the pain and tore her eyes open. It took time for her eyes to adjust to the sunlight, and the pain in the back of her head grew immensely, but once she could see clearly, her heart felt like it had stopped beating. She was still on the loch shore. Her hungover brain struggled to piece together exactly what that meant.

The sun's out, so it's been a whole night. It wasn't a dream. Where is Sarah?

She looked around for her, but she was nowhere to be seen. She saw both sets of clothing still lying where they had taken them off. She looked down at her body and saw that she was still nude and had been lucky the sun was hiding behind the cloudy skies all morning.

She heard the splash in the water again and thought she saw something fly out across the water. She looked toward the area and saw a triplet of ripples in a line to her right. Then, she heard the voices.

"Quit throwing those rocks. The path is this way," a man said.

And then she heard the same splashing as before to her right, only this time she recognized it as rocks skipping across the loch, toward the path she walked down with Sarah the night before.

Wait, they're coming this way?

Alexa looked down at her naked body, then at her clothes at least thirty feet from where she was. She struggled to stand and walked toward her clothes lying by the water. The soles of her feet felt like the pebbles beneath her were stabbing them.

"What kind of fish are we gonna catch here, Dad?" A little boy said from the path.

Fuck, they're getting closer! She bent down and picked up her sweater, shirt, panties, and socks, all damp from waves that washed up the shore overnight. *Aren't my pants here?* She looked back to where she had made out with Sarah, and sure enough, her jeans were still there beside her shoes and Sarah's blouse. Limping from the foot pain, she walked to the pants and bent to pick them up. When she stood straight, she saw the man, fishing poles in his hand and a tackle box in his son's. They stood at the entrance of the pathway and stared at her.

"Hey!" She yelled and covered what she could of herself with the clothes in her hands.

"Sorry, uh …" The man covered his son's eyes but kept staring.

"Turn around, you old creep!"

"Right, sorry." The man spun his kid around and walked back down the path.

"Dad, I think I love fishing." The kid looked back at her.

"We are *never* telling your mother about this." The father grabbed his head and pulled his face back toward the path.

Alexa waited for them to turn the corner before putting her clothes on. Her panties were too wet to wear, but luckily, her pants were still dry so she opted to go commando. She slipped them on, as uncomfortable as it may have been, then put her socks on; the feeling of them being moist disgusted her. She slipped into her shoes to get her feet off the pebbles, then pulled her tank top over her head; the cool, wet tank top felt much better than the socks. She didn't want to wet her sweater, but one look at her chest decided that going without it wasn't an option.

She could almost hear Brooke's sarcastic voice in the back of her head saying, "Are wet t-shirt contests still a thing?" She pulled her arms through her sweater sleeves and wrapped them tightly around her, covering the front of her torso as best she could. *What do I do about Sarah's clothes?*

"Sarah!" She yelled. No response.

Fuck. She decided to leave the clothes where they were and get help. She walked as fast as her body would let her through the path, then climbed back up the hill to the street. Once her eyes caught sight of the pub, she saw a police car outside with its lights on.

They must be looking for us! Alexa ran across the street and pushed through the pub door. Inside, she recognized Christine, Kelly, and Chuck from the night before. They were talking to two police officers, an older man and a younger woman that looked too young to be an officer.

Christine spotted Alexa and pointed her way. "There's Alexa!"

The flight attendants and the police officers walked toward her together.

"Oh, you look awful, dear," Kelly said.

"What happened to you?" Christine asked.

"Where's Sarah?" Chuck asked. The five of them sat silently, awaiting a response. The cops were holding handheld notepads and pens.

"I ... I don't know," Alexa stammered.

"What do you mean you don't know?" Chuck asked, more aggressive than Alexa appreciated.

"Last night, we ... she just disappeared."

"What? How? Where? What were you doing?" The male cop asked. Alexa read his name tag: Officer Brown.

"We went down to the loch, and we ... went swimming."

"You went swimming?" The female cop asked. Her name tag read: Officer Campbell.

"You didn't even have bathing suits on. What did you wear?" Christine asked.

"Nothing."

Kelly chuckled.

"It was fucking cold last night," Chuck said, "You mean you guys *actually* went skinny dipping? That water must have been freezing."

"I know. It was her idea. I didn't like it either."

"And you're saying she just disappeared? What, in the water?" Officer Brown asked.

"Yeah, one second she was there, the next she wasn't."

"Just like that?" Officer Brown asked.

"Where have you been all night?" Officer Campbell asked.

"We were really drunk, and I passed out."

"Maybe she just ditched you," Officer Brown proposed.

"No, if she did that, she would've come to the hotel," Kelly said.

"Her clothes are still where she left them. If she did leave me, she'd be ... exposed," Alexa said.

"Can you show us where all this happened?" Officer Brown asked.

"Of course." Alexa led them to the exit, where the officers stopped the flight attendants.

"I'm sorry, but you'll have to wait here. This is potentially a criminal investigation, and we can't have anyone else interfere," Officer Brown said.

"Okay, we'll wait here," Chuck agreed.

Alexa led the officers outside, across the street, down the hill, along the path, and to the beach. "This is where we were."

"Okay, you just wait here while we have a look around," Officer Campbell said.

Alexa sat on the ground near the path entrance while watching the two officers investigate. They first approached the pile of clothing in front of them; Officer Brown picked up Sarah's jacket and analyzed it, looking for any signs of blood or scratches. Alexa didn't take offense to it; she could understand if they thought there was a fight between the two of them. And it made sense for her to be a suspect in the disappearance since she was the last person to see Sarah alive. She hoped their investigation here would be enough to cross her name off their list, but even more than that, she hoped they would find a clue.

Officer Campbell picked up and went through Sarah's purse, took out her wallet, and checked the ID. "It's hers."

Officer Brown approached the scene where Sarah stripped off her jeans and panties. He dug through her pockets and removed a cell phone. "It's dead. If we charge it, maybe we can find something in her messages."

Both officers met at the water and looked outward. They talked quietly amongst themselves; Alexa couldn't make out anything before they turned and walked toward her, collecting all of Sarah's belongings along the way.

"Okay, well, if your story checks out, we will have to get a search team out on the loch. I hate to say it, but there's no way she would've survived in the water overnight. We will put some posters up around town and keep our ears open for any stories about a naked woman showing up somewhere. If she's alive, we'll find her, and if not, well ..." Officer Brown dropped his gaze to his feet.

"I'll keep my hopes up," Alexa said.

"Let's walk you back to the pub," Officer Campbell said, leading the way.

"Okay, can we leave you here? We want to get started on this investigation as soon as possible." Officer Brown asked as they approached the door to the pub.

"Yes, please. Go find her," Alexa said.

"Okay, if you don't mind, would you tell us where you're staying while you're here? In case we need to ask you any more questions."

"Of course." Alexa pointed past the pub to the top of the hill, where the wall surrounding Bradley's castle stood tall. "I'm staying there."

"Really? Alright, well, we'll be seeing you." Officer Brown nodded and held the door open for Officer Campbell before exiting himself.

"Alexa!" Brooke yelled, and before Alexa could turn back their way, they embraced her in a tight hug. "You look awful!"

"Thanks." Alexa pulled away from her.

"No, really," Marcus said.

"You had us so worried," Elizabeth said. "They told us what happened."

"I'm not the one to worry about right now, unfortunately." Alexa looked past them to the approaching flight attendants.

"I assume that means they didn't find her," Chuck said.

"No, they didn't."

The flight attendants' faces turned to sorrow.

"Hey, at least they didn't find a body," Kelly said, "There's still hope."

"I'm just worried about her son," Christine said.

Alexa's heart sank. *I forgot about her son! She better be okay.* "They'll start an official search party and look for her on the water. They said to keep our ears open for a naked woman turning up somewhere around here. Other than that, there isn't anything else we can do."

"Did she say naked?" Brooke asked Marcus quietly.

"Well, we have a plane to catch. Can I give you my number and have you call me as soon as you hear anything?" Christine asked.

"Yes, of course," Marcus said. He stepped out of the way so Brooke could offer her phone to Christine to add her number.

"Please, let us know. I hope nothing happened to her, but I'm glad you're okay." Kelly hugged Alexa.

"Thank you. You guys have a safe flight home."

The group exchanged goodbyes, and watched the flight attendants exit the pub, their faces spelling sorrow.

"Are you okay?" Elizabeth placed her hand on Alexa's shoulder. "Is your shirt wet?"

"Yeah, it is, and no, I'm not. I need a shower, and then we need to help look for Sarah."

"How are we gonna do that?" Brooke asked.

"I don't know yet, just … can we go home? I need to process everything."

"Yeah, of course." Marcus led the way to the car.

Chapter 8

Let's Investigate

"Do you feel better?" Elizabeth asked Alexa once she joined them in Bradley's bar. Her hair was wrapped in a towel, and her skin still had droplets of shower water resting on it. She wore an oversized t-shirt and sweatpants and hadn't put on makeup yet.

"Have the police come by? Have you heard anything?" Alexa leaned against the doorway and slid down the wall until she was seated, holding her knees to her chest.

"Not yet, no," Marcus said.

"But they will soon, I'm sure." Elizabeth placed her hand on Alexa's shoulder.

Alexa sighed and buried her face in her knees.

"So ... can we talk about what happened last night?" Brooke asked.

Marcus nudged her and gave her a dirty look, shaking his head.

"What about it?" Alexa turned her head so that one eye was looking out at them.

"I mean, there's an obvious elephant in the room here," Brooke said.

"Brooke, now is *not* the right time for this." Elizabeth tried to intervene.

"Are you, like, a lesbian now or something?" Brooke continued.

"Lesbian? No. I still like men." Alexa wiped her forehead, exhaled, and released all the tension in her shoulders.

"Oh good, I was beginning to worry. Those flight attendants said all sorts of things, and you were very flirty with Sarah last night. I was starting to think you had a thing for girls."

"After last night, I do," Alexa said, leaving a shocked, almost frightened look on Brooke's face. "At least I had a thing for *her*. I've never felt that way before, but it was intense. So I guess that means I'm bi?"

"But ... you've seen me naked! Like, so many times. I feel violated," Brooke covered her chest and started rubbing her shoulders.

"I said I've never felt that way before last night. Trust me. I've never looked at you in that way."

"But now my naked body is probably burned in your memory. Now that you *are* into girls, how do I know you won't think about me when you touch yourself?"

"Really?" Marcus shook his head.

"If seeing you naked didn't turn me on before, you must not be my type, Brooke," Alexa turned her body toward Elizabeth. "Are you as uncomfortable about this as she is?"

"Not at all."

"See? You'll be fine. And if I *ever* wanted to think about one of your naked bodies," Alexa scanned her finger across the three of them, "it would probably be hers." She pointed to Elizabeth. "So, don't worry about it."

Elizabeth felt honored.

"Well, that's just because you haven't seen me naked," Marcus winked.

"Trust me, I have. And it's nothing to write home about," Alexa said.

"I'm sorry, what's going on?" Monica asked, walking Hailey into the room.

"Hi, baby!" Elizabeth spoke with a high-pitched voice like one does when speaking to a child. She got out of her seat and picked up Hailey, setting her on her lap as she sat down again.

"Alexa was just saying how she thinks about Elizabeth while she masturbates," Brooke said.

"Oh, my," Monica said.

"Hailey, don't listen to this." Elizabeth placed her hands over her daughter's ears.

"Brooke's really good at missing the point," Alexa said.

"Well, for what it's worth, I'm glad you're okay." Monica held her arms out, bent down to Alexa's level, and hugged her. "They briefly told me what happened while you were in the shower." Monica stood back up and walked to the bar.

"Wait, so you mean to tell me that you actually went skinny dipping last night?" Brooke asked.

Alexa nodded her head.

"How was it?"

"Cold."

Brooke turned to Marcus, "What do you think? Do you wanna try it?"

"What, so we can disappear too? No thanks." Marcus turned to Alexa, "I'm sorry. No offense."

"Don't be sorry. We will find her," Alexa said.

"The *police* will find her," Brooke corrected. "There's nothing we can do about it."

Marcus nudged her once again.

"We have to help them look. *I* have to help them look," Alexa said and stood up. She took the towel off and let her hair unravel past her shoulder.

"And how do you propose we do that? We are in a foreign country with no contacts, only one phone, no leads, and barely know the missing person!" Brooke exclaimed.

"I don't know, but we have to try."

"You know what, we might have a lead," Elizabeth said.

"What? What do you mean?" Marcus asked.

"I don't know if it's a good one, but it might be a start." Elizabeth started digging through her purse on the bar counter, pulled out a business card, and handed it to Marcus.

"Corey's Boats and Tours? Isn't this that asshole from last night?"

"Oh, I've heard of him! He isn't very pleasant. Many women in the area say that he makes them very uncomfortable, and he can be aggressive," Monica said.

"He was very pushy last night, and how he grabbed Sarah's arm was weird. I know we watched him drive away, but under the circumstances, I don't think it's a far stretch to think he could've done something to Sarah last night. And if what Monica says is true, the guy has a bad reputation," Elizabeth said.

"Is his address on there?" Alexa asked.

Marcus turned the card around and read it. "Yeah, it is."

"Then let's go check it out," Brooke said.

T he sun started to set behind the hills surrounding the loch, and Officer Brown was preparing to wrap up his search for the day and go home. He had been searching the loch alongside Officer Campbell on a small motorboat for hours, and they hadn't come up with anything.

"What do you think? Did somebody kidnap her?" Officer Campbell asked.

"Either that or the American girl is lying. All I know is we aren't going to find her today. How about you steer us back to shore, and we can try again in the morning." Officer Brown got up from his seat behind the steering wheel where he had been sitting non-stop for hours and let Officer Campbell step past him to take over. His legs were numb and tingling with pins and needles from sitting for so long. He didn't want his protégé to see him struggle to walk, so he took the first seat nearest the steering wheel.

"It looks like it's gonna storm tonight," Officer Campbell said, turning the key and beginning their trip back toward the shore. They had traveled far across the loch searching for Sarah and were looking at a twenty-minute ride back to the dock.

"Nah, tonight will just be a light rain. It will probably rain in the morning and continue throughout the day tomorrow."

Officer Brown focused on the water, looking for anything they might've missed or anything new to them.

"That's going to suck for the search."

"Eh, maybe we'll get lucky, and it'll miss us. Even with a bigger search party tomorrow, the rising waters will be detrimental. I'm hoping she turns up somewhere tonight."

"That's some wishful thinking, sir."

"You need that in this line of work. Without it, you won't last the year,"

"I'll keep that in mind," Officer Campbell said. She had only been working as a police officer for five months, and Officer Brown was in charge of training her.

Once she was assigned to him, Officer Brown decided she would be his last project before retiring. He would teach her everything he knew about protecting the public and refine her into being a police officer so good at her job that he'd feel like he was no longer needed on the force.

Spending over thirty years chasing criminals, investigating crime scenes, and witnessing things more horrible than he ever imagined had made him obsessed with making the world a better place. He gave everything for this job. His biggest sacrifice was his marriage; his wife had gotten sick of his long hours, which left her lonely. But the final nail in the divorce coffin was once he decided that he no longer wanted children, because he didn't want to bring life into a world that was so awful. She had declared him insane and an awful husband, so she left him. It didn't take long for her to find another man, wealthier tha n Officer Brown, and with enough time on his hands to keep her entertained and give her a baby.

But that was years ago. Officer Brown's body was wearing down, and he was becoming forgetful. He knew that he couldn't save his city like he wanted to anymore, and along came Officer Campbell. She was a bright, young candidate coming out of the police academy. She had breezed through all the psychological and educational tests required for the job and needed some extra time and training to pass the physicality portion, but her motivation drew Officer Brown's attention.

He took her under his wing and gave himself one year to teach her everything, and then he would retire. He would go to his ex-wife, who was now widowed, and try to earn her back. He wasn't excited about the potential of raising a stepchild, but they were close to the age of adulthood, so he figured they would be out of the house soon enough. This plan of his became a new obsession, and even though he knew his wife taking him back would be a long shot, he was always a wishful thinker.

"If she doesn't turn up tonight, be at the office early in the morning, around six thirty, and be ready for a full day of this." Officer Brown pointed around the water. "Don't forget to bring a jacket."

"I'm off tomorrow," Officer Campbell said. "So are you."

"I don't take time off when people are missing like this. I couldn't sleep, knowing they could be dying while I'm at the house." He turned and looked at her.

"You can't save everybody," Officer Campbell said. If it had been anybody else, he would've taken offense to what she said, but she had gotten to know him more than anyone else had during his long career. He used her as his personal stability icon, someone to bring him back down to Earth and remind him not to put so much pressure on himself.

"You're right. But if you come in, you get overtime. You like money, right?" Officer Brown said.

She laughed, and the wheel jerked in her hand. She looked nervous and slowed the boat down.

"Woah, careful there," Officer Brown said.

Officer Campbell stopped the boat and looked at the steering wheel, confused.

"What happened?"

"I'm not sure. It felt like something tugged at it." She looked over her side of the boat.

Officer Brown looked over his side, but the water was too murky to see anything. "It was probably a plant or something. Don't worry about it. Start it up again, and let's get out of here before it gets too dark."

She turned the key in the ignition, and the motor made a stuttering sound but failed to start.

"Try it again," he said.

She turned the key once more to the same result. Then she tried again. And again.

"Here, let me try," he got up and felt the pins and needles in his leg again but played it off like the boat's motion made him look uncoordinated. She got out of her seat and traded spots with him. He turned the key, and the motor started without fail. "See, that wasn't so hard."

"Whatever, just get us home," she said, but before they could move, the motor started getting louder and louder until it sputtered and gave out. "What did you do?"

"I didn't do anything!" He exclaimed, turning the key. But now the motor wouldn't make any noise at all.

"You're joking, right? We are in the middle of the loch!" She yelled.

"Hey, we'll be fine. I'll call for someone to come help us." He reached to the back of his belt where his walkie-talkie should've been attached, but the spot was empty.

"Tell me you have it," she said.

"Okay, I have it," he sat back down. "But I actually don't. I must've left it at that damn pub."

"What are we gonna do?"

"We are gonna have to row the boat with our hands."

"Seriously?"

"Seriously." Officer Brown reached his right hand into the water and looked back to Officer Campbell to ensure she did the same. They ran their hands back along the water, pushing the boat forward.

"This is gonna take forever," she said.

"Tell me when you have a better plan."

After a couple of dozen pushes, Officer Campbell screamed and pulled her hand out from the water.

"What? What is it?" Officer Brown asked.

"I felt something!"

"Yeah, the water. Keep pushing. I can't do it myself."

"No, my hand touched something slimy."

"It was probably the same plant that broke our damn motor."

"This wasn't a plant. This felt ... solid."

"Well, whatever it was—" Officer Bradley's sentence fell short as something hit the boat's underside.

"What was that?" Officer Campbell asked, looking frantically over the edge of the boat.

"There!" Officer Brown pointed to the propeller beneath the motor; it was tangled with dark hair, and something was attached to it. He pulled out a pocketknife and bent down, cutting the hair until it separated from the propeller and released a corpse, which floated up to the surface, startling both officers.

Officer Campbell screamed, "What the hell?"

"I think we found Sarah." Officer Brown looked back at the body to confirm his suspicion. It was a naked woman floating face down in the water. She didn't look badly decomposed, as though she had been in the water for too long. She appeared to be fresh. Except her right leg was completely missing from what looked like one giant bite. "Holy shit ... help me get her on the boat." He reached into the water and waited for her to drift toward the boat, close enough for him to grab her by the arm. "Are you going to help?" But Officer Campbell was not on the boat.

"Where'd you go?" He scanned the water, but she wasn't anywhere in sight. "Hello? Now's not the time for games!" The air was still and quiet. He knew that he was alone. "Grace!" He called for Officer Campbell by her first name. This was his first time using it. He never thought it was professional to call her that, knowing how hard she worked to earn the title of Officer Campbell. "Grace, where are you?"

Something hit the boat, rocking it back and forth, and caused him to let go of the corpse. He waited, hoping Officer Campbell would poke her head out of the water and reveal that she was pranking him, but he knew she wouldn't, especially with the body floating behind them.

Something rocked the boat again, this time much harder, sending Officer Brown over the edge and flipping the boat upside down on top of him. He tried to kick his feet to swim upward, but something sharp snatched his left leg and stabbed deep into his thigh. He kicked downward, but his foot slipped off the surface of what took hold of him. He looked toward it, but the murkiness of the water prevented him from seeing his hand in front of his face.

Only a few more months until retirement, he thought to himself, and those thoughts turned to dreams of a better time as he became delirious from the loss of blood. He dreamt of a love-filled life with his ex-wife, which he missed out on by being too attached to his work. He dreamt of helping her with pregnancy and being there in the room while she gave birth to his daughter. He dreamt of Grace being there to babysit while he left for a honeymoon that he never got the chance to go on. For those last few moments of his life, he believed he was somewhere else, without regret and happy.

Chapter 9

A Day on the Water

As they approached the small dockside building with the worn-down sign for "Corey's Boats and Tours," Alexa said, "If he did something to Sarah, I swear to God...."

"I know, but let's just be calm and see if we can get any info from him first," Elizabeth said.

"It's cold out here, Mommy," Hailey said, tugging at Elizabeth's shirt.

"I know, baby, but I told you to wear a sweater."

"Just be careful around this guy. Don't let him know we're skeptical of him but be skeptical." Marcus held the door open, and they all walked in.

The interior seemed smaller than it looked from the outside; the walls were empty, minus the window behind the front desk that looked outward to the docks and the bathroom door to the right of the desk.

Corey, who they recognized from the night before, sat behind the front desk and spoke with a young man who handed him a key and left the building through the door behind them. Corey finished putting away some paperwork and finally noticed them standing there. "Americans! How can I help you?"

"You remember us?" Marcus asked.

"Of course I do. I never forget a face! What are you all looking for today? A tour of the loch? Boat rental? Jet ski? I have it all, forty percent off, just for you."

"No, I think we're okay. We just have a few questions," Elizabeth said.

"Yes, anything—"

"That girl from last night," Alexa interrupted, "that girl whose arm you grabbed. You remember her?"

"What? No, I don't remember touching anybody. But who knows? I was very drunk." He smiled at Marcus, who did not reciprocate. "But, if you're talking about the pretty one you were with, I remember her."

"Yep, that girl," Elizabeth said.

"Her name is Sarah, and she went missing last night. Out on the water, just shortly after we saw you," Alexa said.

"What? Oh no, I'm so sorry to hear that!"

"We were wondering if you knew anything about what happened to her," Brooke said.

"No, I haven't heard anything. People don't tell me much. I don't really have the best reputation around here, but," he looked around and noticed they were all looking at him, "well, surely you guys don't think I had something to do with it! I would never hurt a pretty girl like that! Unless she asked for it, of course. And I mean literally, asked me to hurt her in a, you know ... sexual way."

"Yeah, we got that," Marcus said.

"Okay, look. I don't know what happened to your friend, but I would love to help look for her! We can take my yacht out on the loch. It's a small one, but it's quick. We can cover the whole loch quickly and see if we can find her! Completely free of charge, I'll drive. Tips are optional."

Elizabeth looked at the rest of them. "Do you mind if we talk it over quickly?"

"No, please, go ahead." He waved them off.

They walked to the corner of the room and whispered.

"What do you think? Do we trust this guy?" Brooke asked.

"No, absolutely not," Marcus said.

"I agree, but I don't think taking him up on his offer is a bad idea. We will be around him more and see if he is any more suspicious, plus we can look for Sarah in the process," Alexa said.

"I don't know about you guys, but I am *not* stepping on that boat. I don't trust this guy," Marcus said.

"Good, then you can watch Hailey," Elizabeth said. "I don't trust him enough to bring her aboard."

Hailey looked up at her and pouted.

"What? No, you can stay back and watch her yourself," Marcus said.

"But you just said you don't want to go, and I can look out and study the ... turtles while I'm out there," Elizabeth said.

"Okay, fine. Brooke and I will stay behind while you two go get kidnapped by Corey."

"What, and miss out on riding on a yacht? Not today. I'm going with them," Brooke said.

"Then it's settled," Alexa said.

"What, no, it isn't—" Marcus protested, but Alexa interrupted.

"We'll go with you," she yelled back to Corey.

"Wonderful!" Corey threw his arms up in excitement.

Marcus looked to Hailey and grabbed her hand, "Let's go get ice cream!"

With little direction, their search on the loch was long and uneventful. Corey brought them near the pub from the night before since that was where the disappearance occurred, but they found nothing. Then, he spent the next couple of hours giving them a tour of the loch they didn't ask for. The tour was just as uneventful as far as their search was concerned, but they did get an exciting view of Bradley's castle from the loch, and Elizabeth made sure Brooke took pictures of it to show Hailey later.

Elizabeth felt on edge the entire time; her prior experience aboard yachts was significantly negative. Alexa was distressed and insisted that he take them back to land, but he assured her they would find Sarah if she were out there. Brooke was the only one of them that felt comfortable. So much so that she removed her top, revealing her bikini, then laid on the white benches on the deck to relax and attempt tanning her pasty skin despite the sun only revealing itself between the clouds every other half-hour. Corey offered the three of them drinks, and though it didn't feel right under the circumstances, they all accepted. Against Elizabeth's better judgment, he did make a fine margarita.

"Hey, do you have a bathroom on this thing?" Elizabeth asked.

Corey sat awkwardly on the chair behind his steering wheel, his butt resting where his head should be and his feet where his butt should be. "Yes, it's just downstairs through the door in the bedroom." He had a contagious smile that made him look like an innocent child, incapable of developing the poor reputation he had. Still, Elizabeth knew firsthand that men could be deceiving with their appearances.

The yacht was much smaller than the one she took with her uncle all those years ago. If she had to guess, it would be somewhere between sixty to seventy-five feet long, with about forty feet of open space on the upper deck lined with benches, a small bar, and a hot tub. On the back end of the upper deck were the steering wheel and a cushioned, U-shaped bench covered by an awning located behind the captain's seat. She wasn't sure if it even qualified as a yacht, but that's what Corey called it, and she wouldn't argue.

She nodded and took the stairs below deck, which brought her straight into a small bedroom. A waterbed in the middle of the room looked queen-sized, with the blankets on top thrown loosely around. To the right of it, along the wall, stood a desk with a swivel chair installed straight into the floor to avoid movement, and on the desk was a lamp and a pile of notebooks and loose papers. Behind the wall was a large window with a beautiful view of the water. To the left of the bed was the door that Corey mentioned. Elizabeth entered and inside was the bathroom.

The toilet seat was cold to the touch when Elizabeth pressed her bare thighs against it. She emptied her bladder in a furious and lengthy stream that burned of alcohol. She cleaned herself up, washed her hands, and entered his room again, where she decided that being a little nosy wouldn't be a problem since Corey was above her in charge of steering the yacht. Her main focus was the pile of papers on the desk. She walked to it and started going through them, most being business-related notes from boat rentals, including ledgers and names of renters. Looking up from them, she saw through the window that the yacht had stopped moving.

Shit, she thought and scrambled to put the papers back where they belonged on the desk, only to drop a handful on the floor. She bent down, picked them up, and smacked her head on the desk's keyboard slide-out tray as she lifted her head back up. She heard something hit the floor and looked down at the miniature, leather-bound booklet that had fallen from the desk. She picked up the book and placed it and the papers she'd retrieved on the desk beside the other documents.

She ran her fingers across the closed zipper that held the booklet shut and thought, *I wonder.* She looked to her right, back to the entrance to the stairs, and once she confirmed that she was still alone, she let her curiosity get the better of her as she unzipped and opened the book. It was a photo album.

She scrolled through the pages of Polaroids that began with pictures aboard the yacht. The photos included women in swimsuits, drinking, and partying. There were dozens of them, some in the hot tub, some behind the steering wheel posing in captain's hats. Elizabeth took notice of the difference in the weather in most of the pictures, indicating that these were multiple events taken on separate occasions. As she got about halfway through the album, the photos became more and more inappropriate. The pictures went from the upper deck of the yacht to the very bedroom Elizabeth was standing in, and the women were no longer wearing their swimsuits. It was also evident in these girls' eyes, the ones that were still open, that they weren't clearheaded. Their eyes were glossy and aimless. As she continued through the photos, Elizabeth became disgusted. Whether or not these women could consent to the images or actions contained within them, she knew that she had no business looking at them.

She flipped through the pages as quickly as possible to confirm that Sarah wasn't one of the women photographed, and as she slammed it shut, Corey spoke from the doorway. "A fan of my work, are you?"

Elizabeth gasped and turned around, leaning against the desk to hide what she was looking through. She gripped the desk with both hands, feeling the sweat forming in her palms.

"You know," he walked toward her slowly and straight-faced; she could smell the alcohol coming from his breath as he spoke, "you could be in this book if you'd like." He pressed his pelvis to hers and reached behind her to grab the photo album.

"Oh, I don't ... no, I'm—" she stuttered.

He held the album horizontally by its back cover and let the pages turn themselves as they fell until they landed on an empty page near the end of the book. "I've still got space in it, see?"

"I'm not one for pictures," she said.

"No? You sure seemed interested in them a second ago. Maybe your friends could even join us." He ran his finger up her arm.

She felt disgusted when he touched her. "I doubt that. We're just looking for Sarah—"

Before she could finish, he grabbed her arms and kissed her neck. She squirmed as chills shot down her spine. His grip tightened, and he tossed her onto the bed.

"We don't have to take pictures, then." He reached down to unbutton his pants, and Elizabeth grabbed his arm before he went further. "What, you want to do it yourself?"

"Either you're really bold, or you're terrible at taking hints. But let me be clear. If you pull your dick out right now, I'm going to rip it off," Elizabeth said.

"Woah, what's going on down here?" Brooke asked, appearing in the doorway with Alexa right behind her.

"What the fuck? Get off her!" Alexa yelled.

He looked Elizabeth in her eyes, his expression screaming confusion and anger, and pulled his hand away. "It's not what it looks like." He held his hands up and smiled. "I thought she was into it."

Elizabeth got up from the bed, shaking her head, and stomped to her friends. Corey started to follow them upstairs, but Alexa glared at him, so he kept his distance.

"He didn't hurt you, did he?" Brooke asked.

"No, he's just a fucking idiot," Elizabeth said.

"Take us back right now," Alexa yelled down the stairs to him.

"Okay—" he started, but Alexa interrupted.

"Don't talk. I don't want to hear your voice. Just drive. You'll be lucky if we don't throw you off the boat!"

Her friends brought Elizabeth to the deck, and they pulled three benches beside each other near the front of the boat, as far away from Corey as possible.

"What happened down there?" Alexa asked, sitting on the bench facing the direction of Corey so she could keep her eye on him.

"I was looking around to see if I could find anything about Sarah," Elizabeth said.

"You were going through his stuff?" Brooke asked, wide-eyed.

"I know, it was dumb. But I found this photo album. It contained pictures of numerous naked women on this boat; not all seemed conscious. I couldn't help but think that maybe Sarah could be in it—"

"Was she?" Alexa interrupted.

"No, she wasn't. Thank God. But before I could put it away, he said he wanted to put *me* in the book. I tried to tell him no, but I was nervous, and he came on strong. Then, he threw me on the bed, and you saw the rest."

"What a freak," Alexa said. "I'm just glad he didn't hurt you."

"Me too," Brooke said.

"Maybe Marcus was right. We shouldn't have come out here," Elizabeth said.

"Can we keep that to ourselves? I don't want to give him any reason to think he couldn't trust me to come out here without him. His inner white knight would make him overprotective for the rest of the trip," Brooke said.

"That's not necessarily a bad thing," Elizabeth remarked.

"It is for me. I love Marcus to death, but he can be so smothering sometimes."

"He can? I didn't think he was the type," Alexa said.

"Trust me, he is."

"It's nice to hear I left Hailey in good hands, then," Elizabeth said as Corey yelled from behind.

"Oh shit!" He turned the wheel hard to the right, and loud crunching and banging sounds came from the front of the boat.

Elizabeth's heart sank into her stomach, and she imagined her uncle's boat sinking to the bottom of the loch. She remembered this feeling as if it were yesterday, and every emotion from that night hit her all at once, most notably the petrification. She felt trapped, in her seat here and now, and within the bones that rested inside her skin. She felt like a terrified child again, she thought she could hear her family screaming, but she snapped out of her trance once she recognized it as her friends yelling at her

.

"Elizabeth!" Brooke yelled.

"Elizabeth," Alexa hollered, "come look!"

Elizabeth returned to the present, where her friends stood at the bow of the boat, peering over the edge. She stood to her feet, but her legs felt like noodles. She walked to the boat's guardrail, her knees quivering beneath her with every step, and looked into the water. They all watched as a group of dozens of sea turtles rose to the surface, some of them bouncing off the hull of the ship but the majority of them swimming around as they passed through.

"We need to get off of this boat," Elizabeth whispered, and then shouted, "How much longer to the dock?"

"Just a few more minutes!" Corey yelled back.

"These are the turtles you were so excited about?" Brooke asked.

Alexa nodded her head and smiled.

Elizabeth didn't look at the turtles with the same excitement. She looked at them with fear.

Chapter 10

Call Me Crazy

"They've sure been gone a long time," Monica said as she hung one of Bradley's cardigans in his walk-in closet.

"Yup," Bradley said from the bedroom. Monica heard him swirling the ice in his glass.

"Do you think they found something?" Monica reached into the pile of freshly dried clothes and grabbed a sweater to put on a hanger.

"I'm not sure. I hope so."

"Me too. That's just so sad to hear about someone missing in a town as small as this. Especially a foreigner."

"It wouldn't be the first time Americans got hurt out there," She heard Bradley slam his drink on the table.

"Of course not, but that doesn't make it any less upsetting." She hung another sweater. "It's been nice having them stay here. Elizabeth and her friends are great." Monica hummed to the tune of "Scooby-Doo, Where Are You!" as it played on Bradley's TV. "And don't get me started on Hailey; she is so cute! I never would've thought I would meet a member of your family, but I'm glad I got to."

Monica awaited a response, but Bradley remained silent. She assumed he had fallen asleep and returned to hanging up clothes until she heard glass shatter in his room. She dropped the clothes and ran in, where Bradley was holding his throat and turning blue.

"Bradley!" She yelled and ran to his side. She pressed the button on his nightstand, which was their "send an ambulance in case of emergency" button, lifted him from the bed, and began performing the Heimlich maneuver until a chunk of ice flew from his mouth and onto the bed. He fell unconscious in her lap, so she laid him on the bed and fell to the floor, shivering in fear. She watched his skin color revert to normal while she awaited the paramedics and watched his chest rise with each breath to ensure he was still breathing.

When the paramedics arrived, she stepped out of the way and answered all of their questions, including what happened to him, what medication he takes, and how she helped him start breathing again. When they loaded him into the ambulance, she made sure the door would be unlocked for Elizabeth when she returned, got into the ambulance behind them, and rode to the hospital.

"Are you okay?" Marcus asked Elizabeth through the rearview mirror as he drove them through the gate to Bradley's castle. It was the first time someone spoke since Marcus picked up the girls from Corey's Boats and Tours.

"Yeah, just being on a boat like that is hard for me," Elizabeth said.

"Did something happen?"

"Nope," Brooke said. "Hey, why does it seem darker than usual here?"

"All the lights look like they're off," Marcus said.

"Yeah, even the porch light," Alexa noticed.

Marcus drove the car around the back of the castle and parked in the oversized driveway. He turned around to face Elizabeth, who sat directly behind him. "Are you sure you're okay? You've looked like someone pissed in your cereal since you got off that boat."

"She said she's fine," Alexa said, but Elizabeth put her hand on Alexa's shoulder as if to say, "It's okay."

"There actually is something that's bothering me," Elizabeth crossed her arms. "But you guys have to promise you won't think I'm crazy."

Marcus nodded, but Brooke looked at her like she was already crazy.

"What's this about?" Alexa asked.

"The real reason I brought you guys here."

They all looked at her, confused.

"We didn't come here to look at turtles?" Brooke asked.

"We did, but there's a reason for it. A bigger reason than writing an article."

"Really? What is it?" Alexa shifted in her seat to see Elizabeth better over Hailey, who slept between them.

"I think I know why the turtles are here. In fact, I'm sure of it. I knew before we even flew here."

"What, are you serious? Elizabeth, that's huge!" Alexa exclaimed.

Elizabeth chuckled though she knew it was no laughing matter. *Huge? You have no idea,* she thought. "I think the turtles are being chased into the loch."

"Chased? What do you mean?" Marcus asked.

"By a predator? What, you think sharks are chasing an entire bale of turtles out of the ocean?" Alexa looked puzzled.

"Not a shark." Elizabeth shook her head, "think bigger."

"A whale?" Brooke asked.

"Stop, are you saying—" Elizabeth cut off Alexa.

"A monster."

Alexa gave her a "you can't be serious" look while Brooke and Marcus shot glances at Lana in Hailey's arms. Brooke ended the silence with a laugh that stopped when she noticed nobody else was laughing with her.

"You're joking, right?" Alexa asked.

Elizabeth shook her head again. "No. I've been looking into this for years, and it's the only thing that makes sense."

"Please, tell me. *How* does this make sense? Do you think there's some prehistoric dinosaur living in the ocean that scares off the turtles every few years? I mean, think about it."

"*I have* thought about it. I'm not sure why it happens, but I *am* sure it does. My best guess is there must be a few plesiosaurs still surviving in the Atlantic Ocean, and every few years, they either get lost or their migration paths come close to that of the turtles, and they chase them here. It would explain why Nessie sightings are so rare and why there were turtles here the night my family was attacked."

"Elizabeth, listen to yourself," Marcus said. "What happened to your family, awful. Nobody would disagree with that. But people think up all sorts of crazy things to push their narrative in a way that their mind can handle, in a way to cope with tragedies like this all the time—"

"But this isn't just some crazy thought!" Elizabeth interrupted. She quieted down when Hailey moved her head to lean on her other shoulder. "I don't know what I saw that night, but I do know that it was something unlike anything I've ever seen in all my research and fieldwork."

"I know. It's just that things like this don't go this long undiscovered. That's why we have scientists. Right, Alexa?" Marcus looked at her, and she seemed to be deep in thought.

"Exactly, *I* am the scientist, and *I* made the discovery. I knew you guys wouldn't believe me if I told you." Elizabeth felt her blood beginning to boil as she worked herself up.

"I believe you," Alexa said, drawing looks from the rest of the passengers. "At least, I'm willing to look into it with you. For Sarah, at least. She deserves to have us check every possibility, no matter how far-fetched."

"Thank you," Elizabeth said.

"But the second we can disprove your theory, we move on, okay? We can't focus too long on this."

"That's good enough for me," Elizabeth said, unlocking her door. She unbuckled Hailey while the rest of them got out of the car. She carried her to the front of the house, coaxing her to wake up, and put her down when they walked inside.

It didn't take long for them to feel how empty the castle was, given Monica and Bradley's absence. Elizabeth thought it was strange, but she shrugged it off. Everyone was exhausted, so they headed for their rooms while Elizabeth went to the guest bathroom and started drawing a bath. She sent Hailey to the bedroom to pick out pajamas to wear, and when she returned to the bathroom Elizabeth told her, "When you're undressed and ready to get in, just twist the knob to the right to turn the water off. I'll be back in a few to check on you, okay?"

"Okay!" Hailey yelled, setting Lana on the closed toilet seat, facing the tub to watch over her.

Elizabeth pulled the door closed as she entered the hallway and saw the front door to the castle opening. Monica entered the foyer and locked the door behind her before tossing her purse to the corner of the room and sitting on the couch.

"Monica?" Elizabeth walked to her. She could see the stress in her eyes when she looked up. "What happened?"

"Bradley. He—" Monica broke into tears.

Elizabeth bent down and hugged her. She didn't have a close relationship with Bradley, even though he was her only remaining family, but she knew he was close to Monica. So much so that Monica probably felt more like family to him than Elizabeth.

"What happened? Did he—" Elizabeth started, but Monica released the hug and answered before she finished her question.

"He's alive, but he's in bad shape. We were talking, and he started choking on some ice! He's in the hospital now. They've got him on a respirator, but they said his brain was out of oxygen for a long time, so they're not sure when he will wake up."

"Oh, no. I should go down there and check on him." Elizabeth stood up, but Monica grabbed her wrist.

"There's no point. They won't allow visitors until he wakes up. All we can do now is wait for them to call me with any updates.

"Okay. I'm sorry I wasn't here to help, and thank you for caring for him."

Monica nodded and licked her chapped lips.

"Come on," Elizabeth extended her hand and helped Monica off the ground, "you've had a long night. You deserve some sleep."

"You're right, though I don't know how much sleep I'll get. I will keep checking my phone until the hospital calls me."

"That's okay, but at least be comfortable while you do it."

"Okay." Monica began to follow Elizabeth down the hall toward her room. "What about you guys? Are there any updates with Sarah? What happened at Corey's?"

"Updates? No. We did run into some of the turtles we're here to see. I literally ran into them. With a boat. But other than that, nothing exciting happened." Elizabeth held open Monica's bedroom door for her. "Oh, and you were right about him. The guy's an asshole."

"Did something happen?" Monica stepped into her room and started digging through her drawers.

"Nothing I couldn't handle. But the guy is a pervert! He had a photo album filled with Polaroids of naked drunk girls he brought onto his boat."

"What? Are you serious?"

Elizabeth nodded her head with a smirk.

"That's disgusting." Monica shivered and closed her bottom drawer with her foot, holding the set of pajamas she had picked out.

"I know, right?"

"What about Alexa and Brooke? Are they okay?"

"Yeah, they're fine. Alexa's still upset that we haven't found anything out about Sarah yet, but that can't be helped." Elizabeth heard the bath water stop running from down the hall. Monica's eyes traveled in that direction. "Hailey's getting in the bath," Elizabeth explained, "I should probably go check on her."

"Okay, we'll talk more in the morning."

"You get some sleep tonight. Seriously."

"You too."

Elizabeth closed Monica's door and left for the bathroom. She opened the door to speak through it, and steam poured through the crack. "Are you okay in there, baby?"

"Yep! I'm getting in now!"

"The water's not too hot, is it?" Elizabeth waited and heard her daughter dip her toe in the water, followed by fully submerging her foot.

"No, it's perfect."

"Okay," Elizabeth giggled. She figured there was no way her daughter wouldn't come to the room completely covered in red splotches, but Hailey wouldn't have said anything, even if the water was too hot. She knew that her daughter liked feeling strong and independent. She admired her for it. "If you need me to make it cooler, just call my name, okay? I'm going to be in the bedroom."

"Okay!" Hailey yelled before plopping into the water.

Elizabeth heard the water splash onto the floor; a mess she would have to clean up before they went to sleep. But she wasn't going to worry about it now. She was too tired. She left for the bedroom, slipped into her pajamas, and crawled into bed.

Just a nap, she thought, closing her eyes. It wouldn't have been *just* a nap if Hailey hadn't woken her up. As soon as she closed her eyes, she was out like a light, dreaming again about the night she lost her family, as she had so many times before. Hailey shook her awake around the time the screams started in her dream.

"Did you forget to tuck me in?" Hailey grinned. She was already dressed in her pajamas and hugged Lana tightly in her arms.

"Of course not. Mommy was just resting her eyes." Elizabeth tossed her blanket off of her and walked Hailey to her bed. She held the blanket open so Hailey could crawl underneath, and she threw the blanket over her and let it glide down like a parachute.

"Thank you," Hailey said, placing Lana in the corner of the bed, to the right of her pillow, so she could watch over her and protect her while she slept.

"Of course," Elizabeth brushed the still-wet hair from her daughter's face, "Now you get some sleep."

"Okay." Hailey yawned with her eyes already tightly shut.

Elizabeth walked to the lamp and turned it off with its pull string. She looked at her bed, then returned to the window where the curtains blew with the breeze. She pulled the window shut and focused her attention on Loch Ness.

"I know you're out there." Elizabeth clutched her hands against her chest. "I'm going to find you."

Chapter 11

We Found a Body

Elizabeth woke up to the sound of commotion in the castle. She put on her robe, left the room where Hailey still slept, and walked down the hall to join Alexa and Monica, who were in a discussion with someone at the front door.

"Did you find her?" Alexa stepped aside so Elizabeth could see the young male police officer at the door. It was a different officer than the two Elizabeth saw at the pub. "Did you find Sarah?"

"Unfortunately, Officer Brown and Officer Campbell never returned from their search last night," he said. Elizabeth felt the mood shift in the room. "We sent another team out to look for them last night. We found their boat overturned and deep in the loch."

"Oh my God," Monica said. Alexa said nothing.

"There's more. We still have not found either of the officers. However, we *did* find a body."

Alexa clutched at her chest.

"It is the body of a woman about your age. We believe the officers' boat overturned while they were fishing her out of the water. Unfortunately, the body is beaten up pretty badly. We were hoping you would be able to come to the coroner's office to identify whether or not this is Sarah." The officer held out a card.

Elizabeth took it from him, and on it was the address of the coroner's office and a phone number. She saw Alexa choking on her words, so she placed her hand on her shoulder for comfort and spoke on her behalf. "Yes, of course. Can we meet you down there after we get ready? We haven't exactly had time to bathe yet."

"Yeah, we can meet you there. And if this is your friend," the officer's voice quieted, "I'm sorry."

Monica closed the door behind the officer as he walked back toward his patrol car. She joined Elizabeth in hugging Alexa as she fell to the floor. "Hey, hey, hey," she said.

"Hey, it's okay. We don't know anything yet. It might not be Sarah," Elizabeth said, but she didn't believe the words when she spoke them.

Alexa tried to respond but couldn't get the words to form.

Monica's phone started to ring, so she pulled it from her pocket. "Oh, it's the hospital!" She answered it and stepped aside.

Elizabeth helped Alexa to her feet when Brooke and Marcus entered the room. They must've both gotten up to check out the commotion. Marcus wore plaid pajama pants without a shirt, and Brooke wore peach, satin pajamas. Her hair was almost as messy as the smudged makeup on her face that she forgot to remove the night before.

"Is everything okay?" Marcus asked.

"The police came by. They said the officers never returned last night, and they found a body when they went to look for them. They think it might be Sarah's, so they want us to go to the coroner's office to identify her." Elizabeth felt Alexa's body go almost limp against her shoulder when she said Sarah's name. "I'm not sure it would be a good idea for Alexa to go, so I'm just gonna do it."

"No, I'll go," Alexa said.

"Are you sure?" Brooke asked.

"Yeah, I have to ... for her."

Monica stepped back into the conversation after hanging up the phone.

"Is everything okay?" Elizabeth asked.

"Yeah, they said Bradley's awake, and we can visit him if we'd like," Monica said.

"Visit? Where is he?" Marcus asked.

"The hospital. He had an accident last night," Elizabeth explained.

"But he's okay, and that's all that matters," Monica said.

"You should go see him, Elizabeth," Alexa said. "I will go with Marcus and Brooke to identify the body. I'll be okay, I promise. You need to go see your cousin."

Elizabeth looked at Monica, and she nodded in agreement with Alexa. "You're welcome to join me and bring Hailey too."

"Okay, but if you need me, call Monica, and we'll come running," Elizabeth said, and Alexa stepped away from her, now supporting herself. The tears dried from her eyes.

"I'll be fine," she said.

T he only thing worse than being at a hospital is being at a hospital with a child.

"Mommy, can I have a dollar?" Hailey asked with her face pressed against the glass of a candy vending machine.

"Hailey, get off of there, baby. You don't know what diseases are on it," Elizabeth said.

"But I want candy!" Hailey said, pulling her face away from the glass, leaving behind her foggy breath marks that blurred the view of the Snickers.

"I know, but now isn't the time for that." She grabbed Hailey's hand and led her further down the halls. *Room 310*, she mentally reminded herself. That was the room number Monica gave before she had to leave her to take Hailey to the bathroom.

She counted the door numbers out loud while she walked past them "302 ... 304 ... 306 ... 308 ... and ..."

"Mommy, I don't like how it smells here," Hailey interrupted.

"310." She stopped in front of Bradley's door. "Trust me, baby, nobody likes the smell." She knocked on the door and pushed it open with the palm of her hand since it didn't have a knob.

"Lizzy!" Bradley smiled when they stepped in.

Hailey ran right past Elizabeth and hugged Bradley.

"Careful honey," Elizabeth said, her arm extended as though she tried to catch her before she could jump on him but failed.

"Woah, I didn't see you there!" Bradley said, catching his breath while she squeezed him. He hugged and rocked her back and forth like an excited grandparent does when they get a long overdue visit with their grandchild.

Hailey let go and slid down the side of the hospital bed to stand on the floor.

"I'm glad you guys came. Monica told me the police might've found your friend," Bradley said.

"Of course. Monica scared me last night when she told me what happened." Elizabeth playfully slapped his shoulder with the back of her hand before sitting in the chair beside Monica's. "You have to be more careful."

"What happened to you?" Hailey asked.

"Alcohol happened. Remember to stay away from it and tell your mother the same," Bradley joked.

"You hear that, Mom?" Hailey asked.

Elizabeth rolled her eyes. "So when do they say you can get out of here? The hospital bed looks about as comfortable as yours at the castle, but I'm sure you'd still be more comfortable with Monica cooking for you at home."

"I'm not sure yet. They said soon, so long as I had the proper care and necessities at home, but I told them I was not in a rush. The nurses are pretty, and the Jell-O here is better than anything Monica's ever cooked for me," Bradley said.

"Hey!" Monica pushed his shoulder, and her phone rang. "Oh, an unknown number. Let me take this real quick." She got out of her seat and left the room.

"I see the two of you get along quite well," Elizabeth said.

"Yeah, I like to tease her. She gets all flustered. But the truth is, I don't know where I'd be without her—" The door opened, interrupting Bradley.

Monica stepped back in and held the phone out for Elizabeth. "It's for you."

"**S**he's in here. And please understand we are not exaggerating when we say that the body is not pretty. After being submerged in water for a while, we believe some aquatic life had gotten to her. We apologize and would not have you see her like this if we didn't need to verify her identity," The officer said, his hand on the steel door that separated Alexa from either a great relief or her worst fear.

She didn't want to believe what the officer was saying, focusing in great detail on the part where he said, "The body is not pretty," because she could never imagine Sarah any other way *than* pretty. She also doubted her ability to handle this situation. It was too heavy for her. She felt like her body wasn't her own, and what she was seeing weren't her own visions to experience.

She felt like she was watching this moment through a TV screen, only she wasn't sitting comfortably in a chair with popcorn and candy. She felt more like she was watching a movie, clutching her blanket, pulling it over her head to protect her from the scary part she knew was about to come. However, she knew the moment was real because that blanket she imagined wasn't enough to prevent the cold that came when the officer pushed open the door. Brooke held Alexa's hand and walked her into the room. Marcus followed just behind them.

The officer closed the door and walked them to the steel slab in the center of the room, where a white tarp lay over the corpse of the unidentified deceased. "I understand this is going to be hard for you. Nobody will fault you for that. This isn't something a person should ever have to do."

Alexa focused on the officer's accent to try and laugh, bringing her back to reality.

"I'm not asking you to look at her for long. All I ask is that you make sure you're one-hundred percent certain whether or not this is Sarah." He placed his hand on the tarp. "Are you ready?"

Alexa nodded, though she knew she would never be ready for this. She felt Brooke's grip tighten in her hand and squeezed back for support. The officer pulled the tarp back, exposing her face, and Alexa went numb. As she feared, it was Sarah. She looked paler than Alexa remembered, and her hair was wet, almost frozen, and matted. She had bruising on her neck and scrapes on her forehead, but there was no question it was her. "Yes, that's her," Alexa managed to squeak out, "that's Sarah." She looked away from the body and noticed how tightly she had squeezed Brooke's hands, but Brooke didn't seem to care. At least, she didn't say anything if she did.

"And you're sure?" the officer asked.

"Yes," Alexa said, and Brooke and Marcus nodded.

"Thank you." The officer stretched the tarp back over her face.

"I was worried. I thought she was going to be a lot worse than that. Disfigured, even," Alexa said.

"Well, that's not the worst of it. Luckily, her face remained intact, but some fish must've gotten to her lower body."

"What do you mean?" Alexa asked.

"Her leg, it's gone. We think some pike must've gotten to the body."

"That doesn't make sense. Would you mind letting me see?" Alexa asked.

"I'm sorry, I can't—"

"I'm a marine biologist. I'm studying the loch here, and I promise that nothing in these waters would be able to bite a person's leg off in under twenty-four hours. I'm only asking because I could probably identify what type of fish we're dealing with here if I just saw the wound. You might have a more serious case on your hands than you think," Alexa said.

"Well," the officer thought for a few seconds with his hand on the tarp at the end of the steel slab opposite her face, "okay. But don't say I didn't warn you. It isn't pretty."

Alexa held her breath while Marcus and Brooke looked away. The officer pulled the tarp up to her abdomen, exposing more cuts and bruising along her body, but the actual damage done was the part that Alexa struggled to look at. Her left leg wasn't just missing. It had been entirely removed from her body with what looked like one clean bite mark, larger than any Alexa had ever seen. A jagged crescent shape originated from above where her left pelvic bone used to be and through her pubic region. That entire area looked like the remains of someone's first day on the job at a slaughterhouse.

Alexa closed her eyes and covered her mouth when she started salivating in a rush of nausea. When she could speak without vomiting, she said, "Please, cover her up."

"Sorry!" He rushed to throw the tarp back over her, missing a couple of times in the process. "What do you think?"

"I need to make a phone call," Alexa said. She walked out of the room, pulling Brooke with her. "Let me use your phone. We have to call Elizabeth."

"Oh, okay. Is everything alright?" Brooke asked.

"Yeah, it's just—" Alexa stopped when the officer entered the room behind Marcus. She didn't want him to hear her sound crazy if she mentioned that Elizabeth might be right about her Loch Ness Monster theory. "I need her opinion."

Brooke went through her contacts, pulled up Monica's, and handed the phone to Alexa. Alexa pressed the call button, and as the phone rang, she exited the coroner's office.

"Hello?" Monica answered.

"Hey Monica, sorry to bother you. Can I talk to Elizabeth?" Alexa asked, conscious of how flustered she must have sounded.

"Yeah, of course. Is everything okay? Was the body—"

"Yes, it was Sarah. And no, I'm not okay, but I will be. Just please, let me talk to Elizabeth."

"Oh, I'm so sorry. Here, let me hand her the phone."

Alexa hoped that she didn't come off as rude to Monica. She didn't mean to, but she also knew that Monica wouldn't be offended after hearing that Sarah was confirmed dead.

"Hey, what's going on?" Elizabeth asked when she picked up the phone.

"It's Sarah. She—"

"Oh my gosh, that's awful."

"I know, but I need you to listen to me for a second. Her body … it was torn apart."

"What? Torn apart? What do you mean?"

"Something got to her. Something in the water. Something big."

"Are you serious? How do you know?"

"A bite mark. A fucking *big* bite mark. It took her whole leg."

"How do you know it was a bite? They found her near an overturned boat. Are you sure she didn't just get caught in the propeller?"

"I've seen bite marks before—studied them, even. Trust me, this was a bite, and it was bigger than any I've ever seen. You understand what I'm getting at, don't you?" Alexa asked.

"Yeah, I do," Elizabeth said. Static rang through the phone, just for a second.

"So what do we do?"

"Tell the officer that you believe the bite is from a shark. Tell them you think one could've gotten lost in the Atlantic Ocean and found its way here. Tell them you suggest getting a search party on the water, the biggest one they can muster, to hunt it down and look for their missing officers. Tell them it is an invasive species and could ruin the entire ecosystem if left unchecked. Tell them it needs to happen today! Then, meet me at the castle."

"Are you sure? If we're right about this, wouldn't having all of these people on the water be dangerous?" Alexa asked.

"Dangerous? Yes. But at least that way, there will be witnesses *if* things go south. This monster will not go unseen another night." Elizabeth said, her voice more serious than Alexa had ever heard before. "Do it for Sarah."

Alexa thought about it. Her stomach churned with anxiety, but her hands shook with anger. They would find out tonight what happened to Sarah, monster or not. "Okay, see you soon."

Chapter 12

Let's Go Hunt a Monster

Elizabeth hurriedly approached the front door, startling Alexa, Brooke, and Marcus from the castle bar. Alexa got out of her seat and met her in the foyer, but she had to hustle to keep up with Elizabeth's pace as she power-walked down the hallway toward her bedroom.

"Are they getting a search party together?" Elizabeth asked.

"Yeah," Alexa said, out of breath.

"How'd they take it?" Elizabeth pushed through her bedroom door and started shuffling through her luggage.

"Take what?" Alexa asked.

"When you told them there was a shark in the loch. Did they believe you?" Elizabeth pulled out a turquoise bathing suit top and slipped her shirt off.

Alexa promptly turned her head and looked away.

"Hey, just because you're into girls now doesn't mean you have to make things awkward," Elizabeth said. "Now, can you help me with my straps?"

"Sorry, I just didn't want to make you uncomfortable." Alexa turned back, and Elizabeth had her bikini top's straps wrapped around her neck, and the bottom straps hung loose down her abdomen while she held the cups to her breasts.

Elizabeth turned around so Alexa could tie the bottom straps around her back for her. "If I was uncomfortable, I wouldn't have done it."

"The officer believed me. I think I scared him quite a bit when I said the ecosystem could be ruined." Alexa finished tying the straps, and Elizabeth laughed.

"I guess that wasn't the biggest lie. People don't often consider dinosaurs when considering invasive species, but I can't imagine an ancient carnivore being great for the aquatic life here." Elizabeth returned to her luggage and pulled out the matching turquoise bikini bottoms.

Alexa would be lying if she said she wasn't watching Elizabeth pull her pants off to see if it did anything for her. Perhaps it was because she had just confirmed Sarah had been killed by what was potentially a dinosaur thought to have gone extinct millions of years ago that she felt nothing. However, she did appreciate Elizabeth's ass in her cheeky panties while she walked to the bathroom, but that was just her being envious. For a girl that she knew firsthand did *not* exercise, Elizabeth was blessed.

"Are you ready to go? I'm just throwing this on in case of emergency," Elizabeth said, throwing her panties from the bathroom door onto the bedroom floor.

"Yeah, I don't plan on getting in the water. At least, I hope not," Alexa sat on Elizabeth's bed.

Elizabeth stepped into the doorway, now wearing the complete bikini, stretching her arms high to apply deodorant. "I hope not too, but we don't know what we're dealing with here."

Alexa turned to her side just in time to spot Hailey toss Lana on the floor before she tackled her into the bed with a big hug.

"Hailey?" Alexa asked, confused as this was the first time Hailey hugged her without her mother's prompting beforehand.

"Mommy told me what happened to your friend." Hailey pushed her face into Alexa's stomach, trying to get as close to her as possible. "I'm sorry."

Alexa teared up, wrapped her arms around her, and pulled Hailey closer with her fingers running through her hair. "It's okay."

Hailey pulled away and wiped a tear off Alexa's face. "I didn't want you to be sad. That's why I thought you could use a hug." Hailey got off of her and walked over to pick up Lana.

"That's so sweet, baby," Elizabeth said, digging through her luggage again.

"The hug was perfect," Alexa said, now on the verge of completely bawling. She had been around since Hailey's birth and never felt like Hailey might like her until now. Hailey was always pretty upfront about how she felt and vocalized constantly how she didn't like it when Alexa and Elizabeth would go out and party. She knew that Hailey thought of her as a bad influence, and as much as she always loved Hailey, she wrote off any possibility of a good relationship with the girl a long time ago. "I needed that more than you know."

"Whenever I'm feeling sad, I always just hug Lana. I don't let anybody do this, but you can squeeze her too, if it will make you feel better." Hailey held Lana out for Alexa to take. Only Hailey didn't realize that Lana would have the opposite effect on Alexa.

Alexa looked at the toy with nothing short of hatred. It finally hit her that Hailey had been carrying around this stuffed animal for not only this trip but her entire life. Lana represented the monster that killed Elizabeth's family and now Sarah. Alexa thought it ironic that she would not only have a toy like this but that it was her favorite. Once she got over the irony, she thought how odd it was that Elizabeth would even provide this for Hailey, given that she had this theory about the Loch Ness Monster for *years*. She wasn't sure if Elizabeth had this theory when she bought the toy, but at the very least, she knew that this tragedy of hers happened on the same loch where the monster that Lana represented was supposed to reside. Then, Alexa realized that what Elizabeth had was more than a theory; it was an obsession. An obsession that she wanted to surround herself with, so much so that she bought a stuffed animal and gave it to her baby before she could even talk. An obsession that culminated in Elizabeth bringing her friends and her daughter to a place she believed was dangerous.

Alexa thought *Sarah would still be alive if I was never here,* but she quickly turned that down because she didn't want to start hating Elizabeth. She told herself that Elizabeth just wanted to know what happened to her family and that her theory was so unlikely that she didn't believe there was any real risk. Alexa decided that her emotions were running wild, and it would be best to make it through today and find out *exactly* what was going on before she passed any judgment. For now, she had to keep her first positive moment with Hailey since her birth just that, positive.

She looked at Hailey's innocent face and caught her own filled with scorn. She changed it to a smile, took Lana from Hailey, and gave her a big squeeze, but not a second longer than needed. As soon as Hailey jumped with excitement, she handed Lana back. "Thank you, I'm feeling better already."

"You're welcome!" Hailey yelled.

"Elizabeth!" Monica called from the hallway and rushed into the room. She was breathing heavily as if she had just sprinted across the house.

"Monica, what's going on?" Elizabeth asked.

"I just got a call from the hospital. It's Bradley. They said he's—" Monica stopped herself when she saw Hailey in the room, "not doing well."

"Did something happen?" Elizabeth stood up from her seat on the floor, where she dug through her luggage.

"I think he had a heart attack. They said they'd got him back to stable condition, but I think we should go down there," Monica said.

"He's alive? Thank God. Alexa, what time did they say the search party will be out there?" Elizabeth asked.

"They said as soon as they could. I would guess in the next hour if they're not there already," Alexa said.

Elizabeth mouthed the word "fuck." "I'm sorry, Monica, but I'll have to meet you at the hospital later. Is there any way you can take Hailey with you? I don't want her with us near the water."

"Are you sure? There's going to be a lot of people out there; I'm not sure we even need to go," Alexa said.

"Yes, I'm sure. I need to be there for my family," Elizabeth said.

"But Bradley might need you. It doesn't sound like he's doing very well," Alexa said.

"Yeah, I'm worried he won't be around too much longer," Monica said.

Alexa looked to Hailey to see if she heard Monica, but she was distracted by her toys.

"He would understand. Trust me; he's been looking for answers to that night's events on the boat his whole life too. I'm hoping I can bring him some later," Elizabeth said.

"I know he has. It's just ... okay. I'll take Hailey," Monica said.

"Hailey, baby?" Elizabeth called for her.

Hailey looked up from her toys.

"Monica's going to take you back to the hospital, okay? Bradley needs entertainment at the hospital and wants to see you. I have some work stuff to take care of, and I'll meet you there later."

"Okay!" Hailey jumped over her bed and grabbed Monica's hand. "Just don't take too long with work. If I have to smell the hospital, you do too!"

Elizabeth laughed and nodded to Monica. "Thank you."

"Of course." Monica walked with Hailey hurriedly, and Alexa watched until they were out of sight.

Alexa sat with Elizabeth while she finished putting clothes on over her bikini. "Okay, if you're ready to go, make sure Brooke and Marcus are too. I have to grab one more thing before we go," Elizabeth said.

Alexa nodded and walked the hallway with Elizabeth to the main entrance, where Elizabeth left her to go upstairs. She watched her bounce up the stairs on the tips of her toes until she disappeared into the hallway. Alexa entered the bar.

"Hey, how are you holding up?" Marcus asked.

"As good as I can when my first girl crush gets eaten by the Loch Ness Monster," Alexa said. "Are you guys ready to go?"

"Yeah, we weren't sure what the plan was, so we didn't think we needed anything special," Marcus said.

"Well, Elizabeth, just put on a bathing suit," Alexa said.

"What, does she think we're gonna dive in after the monster?" Brooke scoffed.

"I'm not sure, really."

"Honestly, though, what does she plan on doing when we get there? If the officers are already out on the water, we won't have a way to ask them to let us on their boat. And I doubt they'll let tourists like us interfere with their search," Marcus said.

"You guys, maybe, since you're the big scientists." Brooke made finger quotes in the air when she said, "big scientists."

"Don't worry, I've got a plan," Elizabeth yelled, descending the stairs. When she entered the room, Alexa immediately noticed the large rifle strapped around her arm.

"Now, what are you going to do with that?" Marcus asked.

"What?"

"Don't act like you didn't just carry a huge elephant into the room," Brooke said.

"Oh, you mean this?" She brandished the gun. "You were close, Brooke. It's an elephant hunting rifle,"

"You know what I meant," Brooke said.

"Of course I did."

"Do you even know how to use that thing?" Marcus asked.

"Of course I do," Elizabeth said, aiming the rifle at the grandfather clock in the main entrance room, visible through the bar entrance. "Point and shoot."

"It's a lot more complicated than that," Marcus said.

"I know. I've spent my fair share of time at the shooting range. Now are you guys ready to go or what?"

"Where exactly *are* we going?" Brooke asked. "We don't have a boat of our own to use."

"I know, but we know someone who does." Elizabeth placed the gun over her shoulder and pulled Corey's business card from her pocket.

"You can't be serious. We are not going back to the creep," Alexa said.

"You think he's just going to let us use his boat if we ask nicely? We didn't have the best experience with him yesterday," Brooke reminded.

"I wasn't planning on asking nicely," Elizabeth patted the stock of the rifle.

"You're gonna shoot him?" Marcus asked.

"No, just scare him a little. Let's go."

They arrived at Corey's Boats and Tours around three o'clock in the afternoon, where they got their first view of the search team on the water. From what they could see, there were at least a half-dozen boats, some bigger than others, spread across the water.

"It's nice to see they're taking this seriously." Elizabeth held the door for her friends to enter the building, keeping the gun on her shoulder tucked behind her back.

Corey was on a call on his behind-the-times corded landline phone when they entered. Looking up from behind his desk, he hung up the phone and stood from his seat upon seeing them, "Americans! What, are you here to accuse me of nonsense again?"

"Again?" Marcus asked, but Corey spotted the gun peeking from behind Elizabeth's shoulder before an explanation came.

"Woah, hey, hey, hey! I'm not looking for trouble, okay? What do you want, an apology?" Corey backed against the wall with his hands up.

"No, calm down." Elizabeth pushed the gun further behind her back. "I'm not gonna shoot you."

"Unless you give us a good reason," Brooke said.

"Shut up," Alexa said.

"Ignore her. The gun isn't for you," Elizabeth said.

"It isn't? Okay." Corey stepped off the wall, beads of sweat tracing his receding hairline. "What do you want, then?"

"We need a boat," Elizabeth said.

"What, to look for your friend? If she's still out there, she's gone by now. I'm sorry to say." Corey sat in his chair. "Now go away, please. I'm busy."

Alexa slammed her hands on his desk and leaned over it. "My friend is dead. Have you noticed all of the police out there on the water today? Some officers are dead too. They're looking for the mo—" Alexa corrected herself, "a shark that killed them. We need a boat to get out there and help them."

"And you thought I would just let you take one?"

"Well, if you don't," Brooke approached him from the side of his desk, wrapped her arms around him from behind his neck, and whispered, "We'll tell our police friends that you sexually assaulted our friend over there."

Corey pushed her arms off of him and got out of his seat. "I didn't rape anybody!"

"I didn't say you did. I said sexually assaulted, and you *definitely* did that."

"They would never believe you!"

"Doesn't matter, does it?" Brooke asked.

"What do you mean?"

"You have a sleazy enough reputation as it is. If the police don't believe you, I'm sure some women out here will. I can't imagine what that kind of publicity would do to your business," Brooke said.

"Okay, fine!" He yelled. "I'll help, but I'm not driving for you.

"That's fine. I can drive the boat," Alexa said.

"You can?" Marcus asked.

"Of course. I spend all of my time on the water. I'd have to learn at some point."

"I guess so," Marcus said.

"Now, what kind of boat are you looking for?" Corey asked.

"What are our options?" Elizabeth asked.

Chapter 13

Why Do These Things Always Go Wrong?

Monica felt hysterical, running through the hospital hallways and pulling Hailey behind her. With almost back-to-back incidents that could've killed Bradley, she was trying to prepare for the fact that he wouldn't be around for much longer, only she knew that no matter how hard she tried, it wouldn't be an easy thing to accept.

When she got to his room, the air felt cold. The nurse at the front desk warned her that he wasn't in great shape after his operation and that she didn't think he would make it through the night. The look on his face as he lay in bed made her think the same.

"Monica," Bradley turned to her and smiled, "you made it."

"Of course I did," she cried out and hugged him. When she pulled away, she caught Bradley looking at Hailey.

"Your mom couldn't make it?" He asked.

Hailey shook her head. She looked scared, and Monica realized that Hailey had never dealt with a death in the family before, considering Elizabeth and Bradley were her only family.

"Elizabeth is ... busy."

"Is she now?" Bradley spread his right arm out so Hailey could hug him. She did.

"They found the body of that flight attendant, and she seems to think she died by the same thing that attacked you all on your father's yacht. She got the police to gather a huge search party, and they will help them look for it," Monica explained.

"Really?" Bradley pulled out of the hug with Hailey and placed his head on his pillow, closing his eyes. "I'm sure she'll find it too. I just wish I would be around to hear about it."

"Don't say that." Monica grabbed his hand. "You're gonna be just fine."

"Nurse!" Bradley yelled, and after seconds passed, the nurse came in from outside.

"Did you need something?" She asked.

"Can you please take young Hailey to the cafeteria and get her some chocolate milk?" Bradley asked.

"Yes, of course," she said. She held her arm out, grabbed Hailey's hand, and led her out of the room.

Monica turned back to Bradley.

"We both know I won't be here for much longer," he coughed, "if I wanted to fight it, I'd probably last a few hours if I'm lucky."

"No—"

"Stop," Bradley interrupted. "I'm too tired to argue. Just let me talk."

She placed her other hand over his, clenching it between her palms. "Okay." She inhaled her runny nose and blinked out a tear.

"I'm lucky I've been able to make it this long. I should've died on that damn boat." He turned and looked at the heart monitor by his head as if counting each beat, half-expecting to see when it stopped beating. "Every second of every day has been painful since," he turned back to her, making eye contact which she wasn't used to from him. "You have helped me throughout all this, and I cannot thank you enough. I've lost my entire family, then you came into my life and made me feel like I had one again. You helped me become a better person throughout the final years of my life, and you've made me feel like this life has been worth living."

"Oh, stop it," she laughed, pulling a hand away to wipe the tears from her face.

"I mean it. Thank you."

"Of course. You—"

Bradley raised a hand to cut her off again. "In my bedroom, in the closet, behind the hanging jackets on the left wall, there is a safe. You know the one?"

Monica nodded her head.

"The combination for the lock is the date that I hired you. When you leave here, I want you to open that safe and read the note inside it. Do you understand?"

"What is the note?" She asked.

"Don't worry about that now; just let me know you'll take care of it. Promise me," Bradley said.

"Okay, I promise."

"Now, go make sure Hailey is okay. I want to make the last time she sees me a happy one," Bradley said.

Monica squeezed his hand and let go, but Bradley grabbed her wrist before she could walk away.

"I don't know if I've ever said this to you, hell I probably haven't said this to *anyone* in decades, but … I love you," Bradley said.

"I love you too." Monica smiled and left the room.

She pulled out her phone and read the text from Brooke that said, "We all went to Corey's Boats and Tours to try and borrow one of his boats. Elizabeth thought she would ask him with a gun, so if we get arrested, you know why. If not, see you later tonight!" Given different circumstances, she would laugh, but there was no way today. Her body wouldn't let her. She put her phone away and followed the signs to the cafeteria, where Hailey smiled and giggled with the nurse who had taken her from Bradley's room. Hailey had a brown carton of chocolate milk in her hand, which she drank from a straw. She also had a bag of chips and a candy bar sitting before her. Monica came to the table and sat beside Hailey to mentally prepare herself to go back and see Bradley for what would likely be the last time.

However, just before she got up to leave, she heard the intercom call "Code Blue, Room 310," and she had watched enough hospital drama shows to recognize that it meant Bradley had flat-lined. Instead of grabbing Hailey's hand and walking her to see him, she embraced Hailey in a tight hug and bawled her eyes out while the nurse ran from the cafeteria table to try resuscitating Bradley. But it was too late.

"**I** still can't believe you know how to drive this thing," Marcus said as they stepped on board Corey's boat. It was smaller than his private yacht from before, but it was enough to seat eight people on its memory foam bench seats and have a separate, fancier seat for the captain.

"It's a bit bigger than I'm used to—"

"I doubt that," Brooke interrupted Alexa and snickered.

"But I'll figure it out," Alexa said, taking her place behind the wheel.

"I sure hope so. No crashing my boat. If there is any damage, I'm suing you. And you can add blackmail to the list of charges," Corey looked at Elizabeth. "Damage also includes bullet holes. Be careful, please."

"Yes, boss," Brooke said.

Corey tossed Alexa the key, and she put it in the ignition. With a twist, the motor started. Corey untied the boat from the dock, and Elizabeth watched him as they floated away.

"So, Elizabeth, what's your plan?" Marcus asked, raising his voice so she could hear him over the motor running.

"Find the monster and shoot it." Elizabeth pulled the gun from behind her shoulder and placed it on her lap, staring sharply into the water for any signs of the beast. Even in the daylight, the water was murky and dark, so she paid more attention to the ripples and waves or anything else that might be out of the ordinary.

"That's great and all, *Lizzy*, but there's just one problem," Brooke said, "You're the only one of us with a gun. I mean, what are *we* supposed to do here?"

"I just need your support," Elizabeth said.

"What, moral support?" Marcus asked.

"Just be on the lookout." Elizabeth turned to Alexa, "Hey, get us over to that police boat. We can talk to them and see if they've seen anything."

"Or see if *they* have a plan," Brooke said.

"You got it!" Alexa turned the boat ninety degrees to the right and twisted the throttle.

Elizabeth held the rifle tight in her lap and clutched at her sun hat so they wouldn't fly away when they caught speed. However, the momentum didn't last for long. They went the distance of a football field before the motor sputtered, and all acceleration was lost.

"What the ...?" Alexa twisted the throttle, confused, and the boat made no attempt to catch speed.

"What's going on?" Elizabeth asked.

"I'm not sure!" Alexa yelled, twisting the throttle repeatedly.

Elizabeth placed the rifle gently on the bench, double-checking that it wasn't pointing at any of her friends, and walked to the captain's seat. "Let me see."

Alexa stepped out of the way, and Elizabeth tried at the throttle. Sure enough, it didn't work, so Elizabeth bent down to look at the glass beneath the left side of the steering wheel, opposite the throttles. Nothing was visible, so she used her palm to wipe away the disgusting layer of dust and revealed the gauges behind it. "I found our problem."

"What is it?" Alexa asked.

"We are out of gas," Elizabeth said. Assuming it was accurate, the gauge had dropped below "E."

"No way," Marcus said.

"Are you serious?" Alexa asked, stepping between Elizabeth and the gauges to see for herself.

"Corey had to have done that on purpose, right?" Brooke asked.

"You think so?" Marcus asked.

"I'm not sure. The guy's an idiot." Elizabeth returned to her seat, grabbed the gun, and placed it back in her lap before sitting down.

"So what do we do? How are we gonna get back to shore?" Alexa asked.

"The obvious answer is to row with our hands," Marcus said.

"Yeah, but I don't like it. Honestly, I'm not sticking any piece of my body in this water if I don't have to," Brooke said.

"Do we have any other choice?" Elizabeth asked. "Alexa, there's a glove compartment by the wheel, right?"

"Let me see ... Yes!" Alexa opened the compartment.

"Is there a flare gun in there?" Elizabeth asked.

"Way ahead of you," Alexa pulled the bright orange gun out of the compartment and pointed it in the air. It looked more like a toy than anything else, but it was all they had. Alexa squeezed the trigger, and with another addition to their string of bad luck, the gun didn't fire. They all stared blankly at the weapon as Alexa pulled the trigger three more times, each time only making a *snap* sound.

"Wow," Marcus said.

"Okay, it's not the end of the world. The police are just right over there. Alexa, why don't you honk the horn and see if we can get their attention?" Elizabeth asked.

"Good idea." Alexa dropped the flare gun, sat behind the steering wheel, and said, "Time to see if *this* works." She pressed down on the horn, which was louder than anticipated.

Elizabeth didn't expect it to make a sound at all, so she was happy it did. Once Alexa let go of the horn, they watched the police boat, which was larger than their own, with what looked like a small second story and an interior that the police must have been in. They waited a few seconds, and nothing happened. Alexa pressed the horn again, and they watched the windows of the boat to see if there was any movement, but there w asn't.

Alexa pressed on the horn again, holding it down until Elizabeth couldn't handle it anymore, and yelled at her, "Hey, stop i t!"

Alexa pulled off the horn and rested her head against the steering wheel. "What are we gonna do?"

"I'm not sure, but we'll think of something just ... silently," Elizabeth said. She leaned back, resting her head against the metal guardrail behind the seat, and closed her eyes to think when she heard movement from in front of her.

"What are you doing?" Brooke asked.

Elizabeth looked up, and Marcus, now shirtless, was untying his shoes.

"Swimming in jeans is going to be hard enough. Can you imagine it with my Nikes on? Plus, these are *way* too expensive to ruin," he said, slipping off his left shoe.

Elizabeth knew nothing about shoes but knew these were Nikes because of the swish logo that decorated the side. And, from what she saw at the store, she knew they were more expensive than she would prefer to spend on a pair of tennis shoes. She would only spend that amount of money on some nice heels or boots.

"Why are we swimming now?" Brooke asked.

"*We* aren't swimming anywhere. I am. To that boat over there," he said, pointing at the police boat.

"Why would you do that?" Brooke rolled her eyes.

"Because I can't think of a worse way to die than trapped on some dirty lake with grumpy women." Marcus slipped off his right shoe. "I'm just gonna swim over there and tell them to come help us out."

"Are you sure? I don't think that's a great idea," Elizabeth said.

"What because there's a monster in the water? Don't take this the wrong way, but if you are right, that monster sunk your uncle's *yacht*. This little boat won't stand a chance. I'm sure it's just as dangerous on this boat as in the water. At least if I swim over there, we can hopefully get off the loch faster."

Elizabeth sat and thought of a counter-argument, but nothing came to mind. "Okay, just be careful."

"Yeah, swim as fast as you can, and yell if you feel anything grab your leg," Brooke said.

"You got it," Marcus stood on his seat, looked over the boat into the loch, and dove in. When he emerged from the water, he was already yelling.

Elizabeth and Brooke rushed to the edge of the boat; Elizabeth was ready with her arm out for him to grab.

"Are you okay?" Brooke yelled.

"What's happening?" Elizabeth shouted.

Once he settled above the water and caught his breath, he yelled, "Why didn't anybody warn me it was gonna be this cold?"

Brooke and Alexa laughed while Elizabeth just shook her head.

"Haven't you gone swimming before? Water is cold," Brooke said.

"Sorry, I could've warned you," Alexa said.

"Just start swimming. The faster you swim, the warmer you'll feel," Elizabeth said, but she was just worried about him making it to the boat without getting swallowed up.

"Okay, I'll be right back." Marcus turned to face the police boat and swam, throwing his arms forward and fast, but he moved through the water much slower than Elizabeth expected, given his form. She knew his blue jeans were dragging him down like an anchor.

"God, something about shirtless men in blue jeans totally turns me off." Alexa shivered.

"Watching him swim in them is even worse," Brooke said.

"Can we focus, please?" Elizabeth asked. "We need to watch and make sure he makes it to the boat."

Chapter 14
Mistakes Were Made

After what felt like the most tiring swim of his life, Marcus made it to the boat. He yelled, "Hello!" a couple of times before his freezing lungs stopped him from trying anymore. No response. Before the rest of his body gave out, he climbed up the metal ladder that hung down the "starboard," a phrase he knew from all of the pirate movies he loved to watch, side of the boat.

"Hello?" He yelled once again when he reached the deck, catching his breath. It didn't take long to confirm that no one was aboard. He opened the door and stepped inside the cockpit, a single square room at the head of the boat, surrounded by four walls to make a box shape. There was a space heater still turned on, facing what Marcus assumed was the control panel, decorated with gauges, levers, throttles, and walkie-talkies, most of which he didn't understand.

This should work, he thought, grabbing the walkie-talkie nearest to the control panel with the type of cord that spun in circles along the length of it. He pressed the button on its side and said, "Hello, is anyone out there?" He released the button and waited for a response. There wasn't one, so he tried again. "Hello? My name is Marcus ... We ran out of gas here on Loch Ness ... Also, I found this police boat, and it's empty ... If you could find us, that would help ... A lot." He paused between each sentence, hoping someone would pick up on the other end, but no luck. He looked out the window toward the boat his friends were on, and they all made similar gestures with their hands as if asking, "What's going on?" or "What's up?"

Marcus wasn't sure how to say, "Boat's empty, and the walkie-talkies don't work" with his hands, so he just shook his head and gave them a thumbs down. He looked back down at the control panel, hoping to find something new that might assist him, but something back at his friends' boat caught his eye. He wasn't sure at first, maybe his eyes were playing tricks on him, or perhaps it was from something the girls could've done, but he thought he saw a strange ripple in the water. He looked back up and studied the loch, watching and waiting. It took some time, and he almost ignored it, but it happened again.

Approximately fifty yards away from the boat his friends were on, there was another ripple from something splashing beneath the waves. Marcus squinted and tilted his head forward, trying to get a better view of where it was coming from, only this time, the ripple was closer to his friends than before.

Marcus started to panic. He waved his hands in the air, trying to get his friends' attention, but they seemed locked in conversation. "Hey!" he yelled, but his voice just bounced around inside of the cockpit. The sound of metal clanging on the floor behind him drew his attention. He turned around and saw a square shape cut into the wooden flooring near the back wall. The square lifted from the ground and pivoted ninety degrees upward on its hinges, and a man wearing a police hat emerged from below.

There was a lower cabin to this thing? Marcus hadn't thought to look because the boat was relatively small.

"What the hell are you doing?" The police officer asked.

"I came looking for help. My friends are in danger!" Marcus wasn't sure what to start with, why he was on the boat or that there was a monster about to attack his friends. "The mo—" Marcus caught himself, remembering they were still pretending a shark was out there. "The shark! It's in the water and going after my friends!" He pointed through the window at the boat.

"What?" The police officer climbed up and into the cockpit and looked out. He must've seen the same ripples in the water now showing up more frequently as they closed in on the boat. "Oh, shit!" He rushed to some array of switches on the left side of the control panel and flicked one, releasing a loud horn from above the cockpit roof.

Marcus looked out at the water and saw that the ripples had stopped. *Did that scare it away?*

The girls were now looking at the boat, unsure of what was happening. Marcus waved at them and pointed at the officer. He yelled, "We've got help!" but he knew they couldn't hear him. He turned to the officer and exhaled. *Now, to explain our situation.* "Thank you, sir. But please, can you help us? We ran out of gas on that boat. If there was some way you could tow us back to shore or even give us a ride?"

"I wish I could, but my boat's not working so well," the officer said.

Marcus sighed. *Of course it isn't.*

"I was down there taking a nap," he pointed at the open hole in the floor, "because I don't know shit about these things. I barely know how to drive them,"

"Well, what's wrong with it?" Marcus asked.

"I'm not sure. The throttle was stuck. I couldn't twist it, and now I'm stranded out here since they gave me the one boat with a broken radio system." He smacked the throttle. "Hey, what is your friend doing?"

Marcus looked toward his friends, saw that Brooke had stripped down to her bikini that he didn't remember her ever putting on, and stood on the boat's edge. "No, don't do that!" Marcus banged on the glass and waved, but she didn't hear.

She's coming to see what's up, Marcus thought. "We have to get her out of there!"

"How? This damn boat don't work."

"We have to do something!" Marcus ran back and forth, panicking in the cockpit. He settled on the same switches that the officer had used before. He flicked the same one that had sounded the horn earlier, and it worked again.

Brooke paused in the water briefly until she started swimming toward the police boat again.

Marcus saw the ripples in the water again, only this time, they were moving away from the boat and toward Brooke.

"Which throttle is the accelerator?" Marcus asked, pointing at the many options.

"I told you it doesn't work!"

"Yeah, I don't plan on watching my girlfriend die today." Marcus settled on the centermost throttle, it looked the most like the one Alexa had her hand on earlier, and he twisted. It didn't give at first, but Marcus put all his strength into his wrist. With a loud *snap*, the throttle pushed forward, and the boat started to move.

"It worked!" The officer moved to the throttle and offered to take it, so Marcus stepped aside. "Wait."

Marcus saw the panic in his eyes and knew that something was wrong. He looked back at the throttle, saw the officer had removed his hand, and the boat was still moving. *Now, it's stuck **and** accelerating.*

Marcus looked back out the window for Brooke, and his heart skipped a few beats. Brooke was no longer above the water, and the ripples were no longer chasing her. It was clear that whatever made the ripples had caught up to her, leaving a subsiding splash across the surface in its place. And to make matters worse, the boat was heading straight for the scene. Marcus couldn't move, and he couldn't watch. He closed his eyes and awaited the moment he would feel the boat running over Brooke and the monster, but he wasn't sure what feeling he expected.

Would it be a *thud* against the metal ship? A *crunch* as its bones were crushed? A *chopping* when the propeller got to her? None of the above happened. Marcus opened his eyes and saw that they had already passed over Brooke without a sound, and were now only a few feet from crashing into Elizabeth and Alexa on the boat, pushing fifty miles per hour.

He didn't have the same time to react as the girls did. He saw that they had leaped into the water before the crash. When the two vessels collided, the police boat lifted off the other boat like it was a ramp. He heard Corey's boat scrape the bottom of this one while his body lifted off the ground. The boat slammed back into the water much harder than he slammed onto the wooden floor. He got back on his feet, shaking with imbalance, and saw the officer unconscious on the floor beside him. *He must've hit his head during the fall.*

Marcus looked out the window and saw they had shifted directions and were now heading further into the loch. With the only thing on his mind being Brooke, he did what any desperate boyfriend would. He made his way to the deck and jumped off the boat.

They had already covered a decent distance, so Marcus dreaded the lengthy swim he had in front of him, but he dreaded what he might find when he got there even more. He swam as fast as he could, ignoring how much colder the water felt this far out, and saw the wreckage he had left behind once he got closer. The boat they had borrowed from Corey was now split in two. One half was overturned, and a single girl lay on top of it, though he couldn't distinguish which of his friends it was from this far away. The other half of the boat was now mostly underwater, with a small flame emanating from the engine that remained above the surface.

Marcus took a deep breath and went back to swimming—now only a hundred or so feet from the wreckage—though he had no idea where to start his search for Brooke, as he wouldn't be able to see anything through this water no matter how bad he wanted to. So, he swam to the one thing he could see, his friend atop the wreckage.

Monica *needed* to tell Elizabeth about Bradley, and Brooke wasn't answering her phone.

"We're gonna go find your Mommy, okay?" Monica said, trying her best to stay composed. She was happy to watch Hailey but didn't have it in her to tell her about Bradley's death. She could only handle so much negative energy in one afternoon, and bringing that to a child would only worsen things. She helped Hailey into the passenger seat. She thought it would cheer her up since she was always stuck in the back, and she buckled her in. Monica hopped in the driver's seat and looked at Brooke's last text message again, confirming that Corey's Boats and Tours was where she was headed.

When she got there, she didn't go inside. She followed the angry-looking man that came outside and walked to the dock behind it.

"Excuse me, Corey?" Monica yelled while Hailey held her hand and followed her.

The man turned and looked at her. "I'm sorry, I don't have the time." He continued down the pier, key in hand, and started untying a jet ski from the dock.

Monica hurried so she could get within talking distance. "Please, sir. I'm looking for my friends."

"Everybody is nowadays. Why do they always come to me for help with that?" Corey said.

"Because they said they were coming here for a boat."

"Do you know how many boats I rent out daily? You'll need to be more descriptive than that, sugar tits." He got on the jet ski seat and put the key in the ignition.

Monica's eyebrow twitched at the remark, but she let it slide since she needed help. "You might remember this group. The ones with the gun?" Monica hoped that what Brooke said was true and that she didn't look completely insane right now. But, by the look on Corey's face, he knew exactly who she was talking about.

"Yeah, I know the group. Funny, I'm going over to them right now. Hop on." He leaned forward to make room on the seat for both of them and tilted his head, inviting them on.

"What do you think, Hailey? Does riding a jet ski sound fun?" Monica asked.

Hailey nodded her head and smiled. Monica wished she could remain as optimistic and innocent as Hailey, but she couldn't. It did brighten her day, if even just a little, to see that Hailey could still be happy.

Chapter 15

I Leave It All to You

The way the boat wreckage rocked on the water made Elizabeth feel sick, but not because of her unbalanced equilibrium. She had plenty of nightmares regarding her trauma throughout her life, but nothing made her feel like she was reliving them quite like this. To start, Sarah went missing, then Bradley's health declined, followed by their boat running out of gas in the middle of this body of water that she could only refer to now as a "Hell pool," and the icing on this catastrophe cake: Marcus managed to drive a boat into them. But just before that, she watched one of her best friends get swallowed up in the aforementioned Hell pool. She was glad she couldn't see Brooke's face when she was pulled under. It would be yet another horrifying memory branded on her psyche.

She hadn't seen what happened to Alexa after the crash. They both jumped into the water to save themselves once they saw that the boat wasn't trying to slow or change course from hitting them. After the collision, Elizabeth surfaced and climbed aboard the wreckage, but Alexa was nowhere to be seen. She thought she was alone until she heard a voice yelling behind her.

"Hey, Elizabeth!"

Elizabeth did her best to pivot her body around the wreckage, making sure not to move too abruptly. She wasn't sure how buoyant Corey's boat was in its condition and didn't intend to make it sink if she could help it. She stopped once she saw that it was Marcus swimming for her.

"What the *hell* happened?" Elizabeth yelled. She looked past him at the police boat, still racing ahead.

Marcus paused his swimming to yell back his response. "I don't know! I saw something chasing after Brooke, so I tried to drive the boat to her to scare it, and the fucking thing got stuck."

"What do you mean it got stuck?"

"It got stuck, I don't know! The throttle got stuck, and I couldn't stop it. Did you see what happened to Brooke?" He started swimming, closing the distance between them so they could talk without yelling.

"I saw her ..." Elizabeth revisited the memory of Brooke being pulled under. "I saw her get dragged beneath the surface."

"Fuck!" Marcus yelled. "Where's Alexa?"

"I don't know. I haven't seen her since the crash."

"Did she make it off the boat?"

"I think so. We jumped off at the same time. She just never came back up."

Marcus was now at the boat wreckage. He placed both hands where he could grip, but Elizabeth stopped him before he pulled himself out of the water.

"Wait! Be careful. I'm not sure if this thing can support us both."

"Elizabeth, I'm freezing. I'm not going to die like Jack in the Titanic. I'm climbing on."

Elizabeth braced herself and watched the water against the boat to see if it would go down any while he lifted himself aboard, but he stopped halfway up.

"What the hell?" Marcus asked, not expecting a response.

"What?"

Marcus shifted his lower half and kicked his leg. "I think my foot is caught on something."

"Just kick your leg around. Whatever it is will fall off."

He tried to kick it some more, but it was clear that he struggled.

"I thought I had it, but now it feels tighter." He looked down at the water, but she knew he couldn't see anything. "Seriously, this hurts!" With his last kick attempt, he winced at the increasing pain and looked up to Elizabeth just before his body jerked down, slamming his face into the side of the boat. He tried to scream, but all he managed was a yelp before his mouth filled with water he gurgled as he got pulled under.

"Marcus!" She yelled, but once the splashing of the water faded, she only saw her reflection against the murkiness of the loch, and she knew he was gone. "*Goddammit!*"

She pressed her face against the bottom of the boat she lay on, cowered her head beneath her hands, and pulled her hair. At the same time, she let out a bellowing scream that would have sounded familiar to anyone who has seen a horror movie where the female lead comes across the mutilated body of a friend or loved one.

She was trapped, helpless, and in constant danger, yet all she could focus on was how cold she was in her wet clothes. She thought she was delirious or in shock. Still, she knew that there was some form of a mental defense system engaging within her that wanted her to fixate on something as small as that, to bring her mind away from the fact that two of her friends, possibly three, had been killed by the same monster that took her family all those years ago.

She decided that all she could do was solve one problem at a time. She started with her shoes and socks. She hated the way they felt, soaked against her feet. She pulled them off, and lacking a flat surface to leave them on, she threw them into the water. At first, she just dropped her socks in, but before she came to terms with losing her shoes, she thought tossing them far away would be a good idea, potentially leading the monster over there if it thought something was there to eat. She threw the first shoe not very far, and almost slipped off the boat when she launched the second one as hard as she could.

Next, she slipped off her shirt. She let it rest on the boat beside her, uncaring whether it would fall into the water or not. She rolled onto her back and lifted her feet into the air so she could slip out of her pants and drop them into the water. She was over it. Now, she was still cold when the breeze hit her, but at least she wasn't uncomfortable with the wet clothes sticking to her skin.

When she started thinking about the look on Marcus's face when he got pulled under, she quickly changed her thoughts to: *how do I get out of here*?

She looked out on the loch toward where there were more police boats, but they had all left to investigate the one that Marcus had abandoned, which now had reached land in the distance.

She knew that the police weren't going to rescue her any time soon, so her only two options were waiting it out, hoping the monster didn't try to play with the boat debris she was on, or swimming back to shore, hoping she makes it there without becoming another appetizer on this monster's platter that she so graciously provided for it.

It didn't take much thought to decide that waiting it out on the boat remnant was better. *Out of the water is better than in it*, she told herself. She put her legs down. Now lying flat on her back, she started thinking of a prayer. She was never religious before then, but if a higher power was listening to her, *why not?* Just before she could come up with her request for that higher power, her prayer was prematurely answered. She heard a motor, and it was coming toward her.

She sat upright and held her hand at eyebrow level to provide a window of shade as she looked out to see who her hero was, and it was the last person she would've ever expected. It was Corey, the pervert who was once an object of abhorrence. Yet now, she couldn't be happier to see him. She even had a quick thought about letting him have his way with her if it meant getting her off this God-forsaken loch, but deep down, she knew that she wouldn't let him touch her, aside from helping her on the jet ski he was riding.

And, not entirely to her surprise, the happiness of seeing Corey almost immediately shot to anger because he wasn't alone. Monica was holding on to him tightly, and behind her was Hailey.

"Oh my God, Elizabeth, what happened?" Monica asked.

"Seriously, what the hell did you do to my boat?" Corey asked.

"There was an accident, I'm sorry. What are you doing out here, Monica? And why did you bring Hailey? It's *way* too dangerous out here for her!" Elizabeth said.

"I didn't know it would be like this. I'm sorry," Monica said.

"I told you there was a monster here!"

"I know, but … I'm sorry. I didn't know, and Corey didn't tell me there was an accident out here. I only just saw it when we came around the corner."

"It's okay, just take her back, drop her off, and come and get me after. Please, just get her *off* the water."

"I'm not leaving here without you. You need to pay for my boat!" Corey said.

"Fuck your boat! Get my daughter out of here," Elizabeth screamed.

"Wait, Elizabeth, where are the others?" Monica asked.

"They—" Elizabeth stopped before answering. She looked at Hailey and didn't want to say any horrible details out loud in front of her.

"No," Monica said.

"Wait, I don't understand," Corey said.

"It doesn't matter. Please, just get her out of here!" Elizabeth yelled behind a frustrated facepalm.

"Mommy, Lana!" When Hailey yelled, it was the only thing Elizabeth could hear. She focused on her because it made her happy and brightened her day immediately, even after all of the tragedy. After all this loss, she still had Hailey, which is what mattered most.

"Lana's at home, baby, and that's where you should be. I'm sorry they brought you out here."

"No, look!" Hailey shouted.

Elizabeth pulled her hand from her face and saw Hailey pointing behind Elizabeth's back. She also saw the combined looks of terror and amazement on the faces of Corey and Monica. Her heart sunk into her chest when she spotted half a dozen turtle shells rising out of the water, swimming past the jet ski.

When Elizabeth turned around, Hailey yelled, "It's Lana!"

Emerging from the water, with a neck extending at least fifteen feet above the surface, sat the monster that tormented Elizabeth for all of these years. In all of the nightmares of this beast that she had withstood, and out of all her mind's renditions of what it would look like, she never expected something so beautiful yet frightening all at once.

It was undeniably a plesiosaur, as she predicted. It had soft, scaly skin, similar to the sea turtles that Elizabeth was supposed to study. Its color was bluish-gray, with dark lines decorating its face and trailing the back of its neck, disappearing beneath the water. It had pretty green eyes sitting above a lengthy face with two small holes in a nose. Elizabeth saw steam come from its nostrils when it exhaled its hot breath past the freezing water dripping from its face, similar to how water dripped from Hailey's hair when she got out of the bath without drying it properly. Once she looked closer, she recognized that it wasn't just water, but blood dripping from its mouth that rested slightly a jar.

Elizabeth was too stunned to know what to do without a gun, having lost it during the wreck. There wasn't much she could do, anyway. This creature was giant and its proximity to her was half the length of its neck. It stared directly into her eyes as if looking into her soul. She wondered if it remembered her from when she was a kid but doubted it.

When its mouth opened, she analyzed its teeth. They were long and sharp, shaped similar to a canine tooth, each approximately eight inches in length. It let out a violent roar, unlike anything she had ever heard and unlike anything that had ever been recorded. Its breath smelled of the ocean and decay.

When its neck extended toward her, she heard the yelling behind her.

"Shit!" Corey yelled.

"Elizabeth!" Monica screamed.

"Mommy!" Hailey cried.

The monster's mouth fit right over Elizabeth's head, piercing her spine with its upper row of teeth, and her abdomen, just below her navel with the lower. She didn't even have time to scream. They say your life flashes before your eyes when you're going to die, but it wasn't her life that Elizabeth saw. It was Hailey's. She first saw the moment she held her in the labor room. Then she saw her first steps, followed by the first time she fell over, only to get back up and start walking it off without skipping a beat. She heard Hailey's first word, Mommy, and once again felt the bliss of hearing it. Lastly, she saw Hailey smiling, which comforted her like nothing else ever had.

2

"Elizabeth!" Monica continued to scream, but it was no use.

The monster lifted Elizabeth off the boat, her legs hanging limp from its mouth as blood spilled out, staining what was left of her pale physique. Monica watched the monster play with her body like a dog does when they catch their squeaky toy, ripping it left and right, clenching its teeth tighter, and wringing her body of more blood.

Hailey shrieked like a banshee when the monster tossed the lower half of Elizabeth twenty feet across the water, her internal organs spilling out in chunks and droplets, leaving a red trail of her airborne path before she slammed into the other half of Corey's boat that had been engulfed in flames. The monster extended its head toward the sky, and Monica watched it swallow Elizabeth's top half. She finally thought to put her hand in front of Hailey's eyes so she didn't have to see this.

Monica could see Elizabeth's corpse protruding from its throat as it went down, like when a snake eats something larger than itself. After the lump in its throat was beneath the water's surface, the monster brought its attention to the jet ski. Monica locked eyes with the beast, and Corey must have done the same, prompting him to rev the jet ski's engine. The monster drifted toward them without apparent motion, never shifting its focus.

"We've got to get out of here," he said. He turned the jet ski back toward the direction they had come, and Monica kept her eyes on the monster the entire time.

Corey sped faster than he did on the way in, pushing fifty miles per hour now, but the monster was no longer just drifting toward them. Its head was lowered close to the surface of the water as it swam, and it was coming quickly.

"It's gonna catch us!" Monica yelled.

"I can't go any faster!" Corey yelled back.

Monica transitioned from covering Hailey's face to pulling her head in and covering her whole body as the monster closed in. She heard a loud *bang* and thought for a second that the jet ski backfired like an old car, but when she looked up from Hailey, the monster was no longer coming for them and was now sinking into the water with a big, red, bloody hole in between its eyes.

Monica first thought an officer from the boats that approached in the distance must have pulled the trigger, but once she scanned the area, she saw Alexa standing on a dock, her eyes looking down the sight of the rifle that Monica recognized from Bradley's room. Alexa dropped the gun and collapsed on the dock, and Monica didn't blame her. As Corey pulled the jet ski to that same dock, Monica helped Hailey off, and they collapsed beside her.

Monica spent the next few weeks going to therapy, trying to get the image of Elizabeth getting ripped apart out of her head. She invited Alexa and Hailey to stay with her for a while before returning to the States, but Alexa declined. She wanted to get Hailey back to her country as soon as possible to figure out what they would do with her now that one parent was dead and the other was in jail. On top of that, Alexa was going to need counseling herself and said that "she couldn't take it seriously if the counselor had a Scottish accent."

Once Monica felt like she could function semi-regularly and thought she could handle it, she returned to Bradley's castle and followed his instructions. There were only two things inside the safe. A bottle of whiskey, saved for the inevitable time when he was too unhealthy to continue indulging in the sauce, and Monica would no longer provide it for him, and a manila envelope.

She took both and brought them to the bar downstairs, where she opened the bottle and poured herself a glass with two ice cubes. She turned on the TV mounted in the corner and let the news play as background noise to help her focus on the stressful task at hand. The news was still talking about the same BS that it had been since the day the Loch Ness Monster revealed itself to the world, i.e., six confirmed deaths by the animal in the past month, an injured cop from a police boat crashing onto a beach, an increase in tourism from people coming to see the dead dinosaur that they were studying—leaving it in the water to preserve its body for as long as possible, and of course the discovery that the monster had been pregnant. Because Alexa had given this information in a couple of interviews, the world was talking about Elizabeth's theory: the plesiosaur's relationship with the sea turtles, coupled with the announcement of an oncoming search for more of the "living fossils" in the Atlantic Ocean. This news would've been exciting to Monica if she wasn't involved, but unfortunately, she was.

She took two sips from the glass before opening the envelope and another before removing the paper within. She felt she knew what would be inside, and while she was partially correct, it still shocked her.

It was his will, which was the part she anticipated, but what she didn't expect was what it said: all of his fortunes, every dollar in his bank account, all of the cash he had in the castle, the castle itself, everything inside of it, and the property it stood on were all left to Monica; and the yacht company he owned, all of its worth, and all of its future profits, were left to his only remaining family, Elizabeth and her daughter Hailey. At first, she teared up, not because she knew she was set for life, but because Bradley truly thought of her as family. She was as overjoyed with that knowledge as she was saddened that neither Elizabeth nor Bradley knew the other had passed. And Monica promised herself that Hailey would receive her fair share of Bradley's fortune no matter what happened.

It would never be enough to replace what Hailey had lost, but she hoped it might soften the blow.

Epilogue

"Hang on. I'm almost ready!" Hailey stuffed a sweater and over-ear headphones into her suitcase. She scanned her messy room for anything else she could be forgetting. High school textbooks, crumbled sheets of paper, and empty chip bags decorated her computer desk. She grabbed her waste bin, slid the paper sheets into it, and threw the chip bags on top of them before sliding them back under the desk. She was going to be out of the house for a few months at summer camp and didn't want to give anyone a reason to come into her room and clean it for her.

"You're gonna miss your bus!" Megan, Hailey's adoptive mother, yelled from the front door of their house.

"Just a minute!" Hailey kicked around the dirty laundry on her floor so that it was all in a neat pile beside her bed, on the side where it wouldn't be visible from her door. She looked at her room one last time and focused on the picture she had framed on her nightstand. It was of her mother in the hospital, still in a blue gown, cradling a newborn Hailey. She had many other pictures where she was with her mom, but Hailey was a stubborn child who didn't like to pose or smile, so this one was her favorite. It was the photo where her mother wore her biggest smile. Hailey lifted the picture and hugged it to her chest.

"I miss you," she said, as she had so many times before. She put the picture back where she grabbed it from, extended the handle of her suitcase, and wheeled it to her bedroom door, where she flicked the switch to turn off the light. She brought the bag downstairs, where Megan waited patiently with the front door open.

"Finally ready to go?" Megan asked. Her hair was blonde and wavy, much like Hailey's biological mom's was, and she had the same blue eyes. People never questioned their relationship, as Megan very well *could* have been Hailey's birth mom, but Hailey would take every opportunity to point out that she wasn't.

"If I have to." Hailey rolled her eyes. This summer camp she was going to wasn't just any summer camp. It was designed to help kids like her who have suffered significant trauma or tragic loss and aren't coping well. She didn't think she needed to go to a place like this, nor that she deserved to have her summer break ripped away. She felt she coped as well as possible, having seen what she did. Watching a parent murdered is one thing, but having seen them violently torn apart and thrown across Loch Ness, spilling a blood rainbow across the sky, is something else entirely. Yet, she still passed all of her classes, rarely talked back, stayed off drugs, only drank alcohol a handful of times, and never let a guy do more than graze her breast during a make-out session—that she ended early due to the discomfort it caused because she wasn't ready for something like that yet. But God forbid she gets in one fight at school because a girl made fun of her for being an orphan, and Megan comes to the rescue by sending her off to some PTSD victims camp to make sure that she isn't internalizing her feelings any longer.

"Wait, before you go!" Alexa came running in from the living room with Lana, Hailey's favorite childhood toy, in her hand. "You can't forget this." She handed it to Hailey.

"You had her fixed!" Hailey grabbed Lana from her. During one of Hailey's recent night terrors, she woke up screaming and ripping the stuffed doll, with cotton falling from its severed head onto her stomach. It had been weeks since the incident, and she hadn't known where Lana had gone. She just assumed that Megan had tossed it. "Thank you." Hailey felt like she was going to cry.

"Of course! We know how much she means to you." Alexa stepped behind Megan and wrapped her left arm around her waist, where they clasped hands in a way that their wedding bands shimmered together in the light coming through the front door.

Hailey didn't believe that Megan understood, but Alexa definitely did. Hailey may have had her problems with Alexa in the past, but she and Alexa shared trauma, and Alexa had grown considerably since then. She never thought of Alexa as a mother per se, and Alexa never tried to convince her that she *was* one, given their history. Megan wasn't a long-time friend of her mother's; she came into their life years after Alexa adopted her. Naturally, she did as stepmothers do and overcompensated, trying to win motherly affection from her and pushing her away in the process.

However, she didn't have any negative feelings toward Megan, and she loved how good she was for Alexa—having seen not only the women she tried to date in the years after Scotland but also the men that she had been with before *and* after. She just looked at Megan as a sort of friend of the family that lived under her roof and *hated* when she tried to act like her mother.

"Well ... now I'm ready." Hailey placed Lana on her suitcase so that she leaned her neck between the bars of the handle when she wheeled it forward.

"You be safe out there, please. I know it's not how you wanted to spend your summer, but it will be good for you and could be a lot of fun!" Alexa leaned forward, but not much lower as Hailey was now up to her nose in height, and hugged her.

"And I know phones aren't allowed there, but they've gotta have some sort of landline you can use to call us if anything happens." Megan hugged Hailey next.

"Okay. I'll try to enjoy it while I'm there, and I'll see you both in a few months." Hailey wheeled her luggage through the door. "Oh, and ... thanks." She petted Lana's head.

Alexa smiled as Hailey and Lana continued to the taxicab waiting at the end of their driveway. The driver helped her put her luggage in the trunk, and she volunteered to hold Lana for the ride to the bus stop. She got in the cab's passenger seat and looked through the tinted window at her two moms waving with tears in their eyes. They may not have been the mother she was born to, but she loved and appreciated them. She also knew she would miss them both over the next few months, but never as much as she missed her *real* mom, who she hoped would be watching over her on this next adventure.

Also by Matthew Mercer

It Came From Above

Mysterious disappearances. A helpless group of friends. Will any of them survive?

Sean finally has an opportunity to take his long time crush Samantha on a date. They go to the drive-in movie theater, they're flirting back and forth, and everything is going perfectly. That is, until she disappears.

In this story, reminiscent of classic 80s slasher films, Sean and his friends try their best at finding out what really happened that night, while trying to avoid meeting their own demise along the way.

It Came From the Woods

They agreed to make a documentary. They didn't know it was about their own massacre. Now, Nancy Miller is faced with the impossible task of proving to the world that Bigfoot killed her friends.

Notes From the Author

This book was the hardest for me to write by *far*. With plans for this to be the last in the series for a while, I wanted to really dive in and get used to writing about things I would otherwise be too uncomfortable to write. I tried to really place myself in these character's shoes and understand their thoughts and motivations, given situations that I have never experienced myself (motherhood, sexual identity crisis, major loss of family, etc.). On top of that, this book takes place in a specific location, so I couldn't just make stuff up as I went along like I usually do. Because I have never been to Scotland, this took a lot more studying than I had hoped.

I felt completely out of my zone on this one, and it led to a lot of procrastination and writer's block. I wrote a few drafts that I hated so much that they never got an ending. Once I was writing this story for the third time, I still didn't know what was even going to happen, and it *really* frustrated me. This book started to feel like a chore, and more of something that I wanted to get out of the way, rather than something I once was so excited to work on (seriously, when I first started this book I was so obsessed that I was typing it on my phone behind the cash register at work in between customers).

I stepped away from this story for so long that I started think-ing about new ones. I came up with the concept for my first full-length novel, and started plotting it out, along with another novel with a concept I've been letting marinate for a while. I created a whole back log of stories to write, and a road map for where these books will go for the next few years, all before I ever thought of how this one would end.

Eventually the ending did come to me, and I used it to write an outline for the first time, which gave me the motivation needed to push through and finish this thing. Overall, I am happy with the finished product, and I hope you readers are too, because this story was very close to being left untold.

www.ingramcontent.com/pod-product-compliance
Lightning Source LLC
Chambersburg PA
CBHW020037310726
48970CB00007B/2296